BLACK HILLS
ATONEMENT

BLACK HILLS
ATONEMENT

A NOVEL

Jane Iwan

atmosphere press

Published by Atmosphere Press

Cover design by Matthew Fielder

Atmospherepress.com

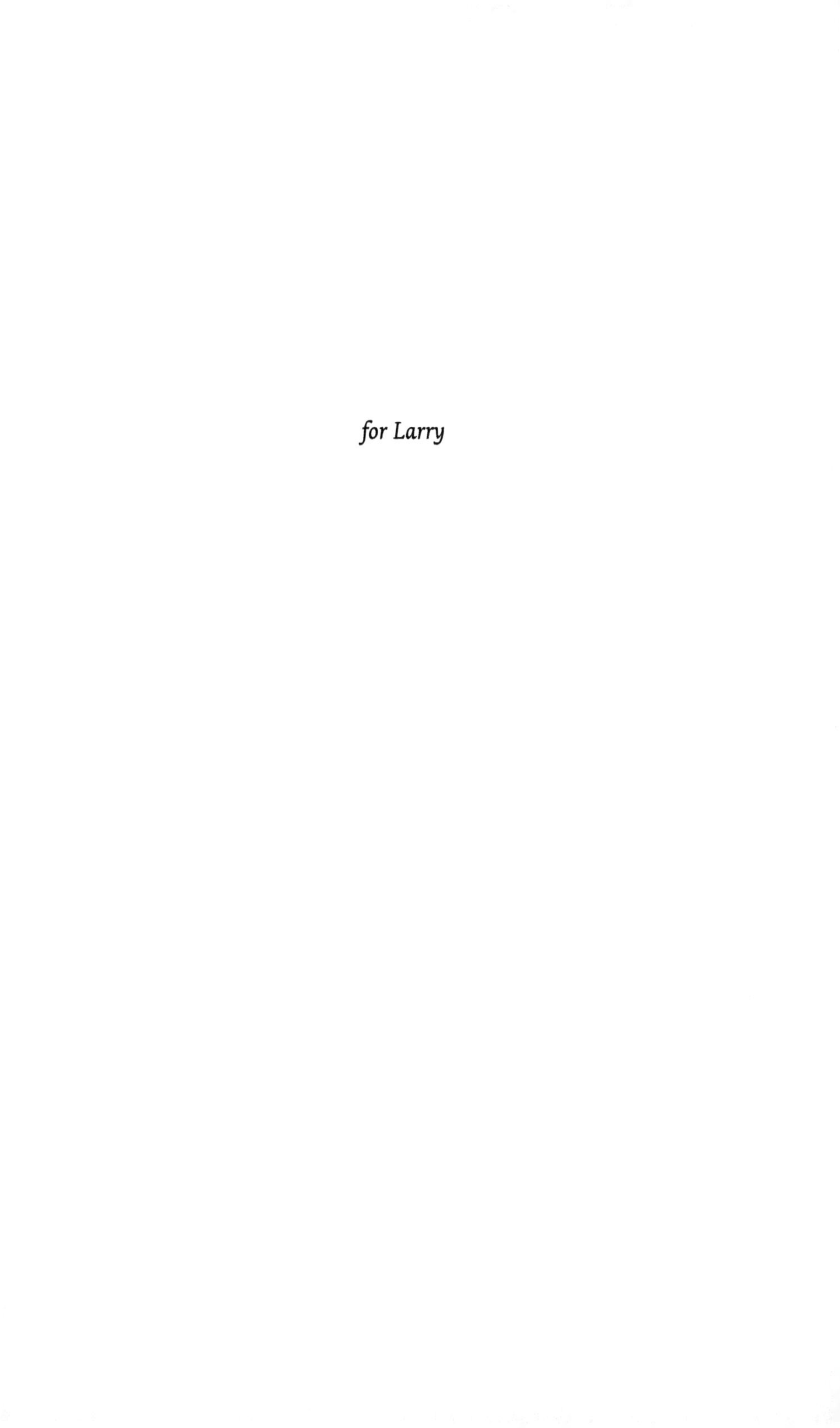

for Larry

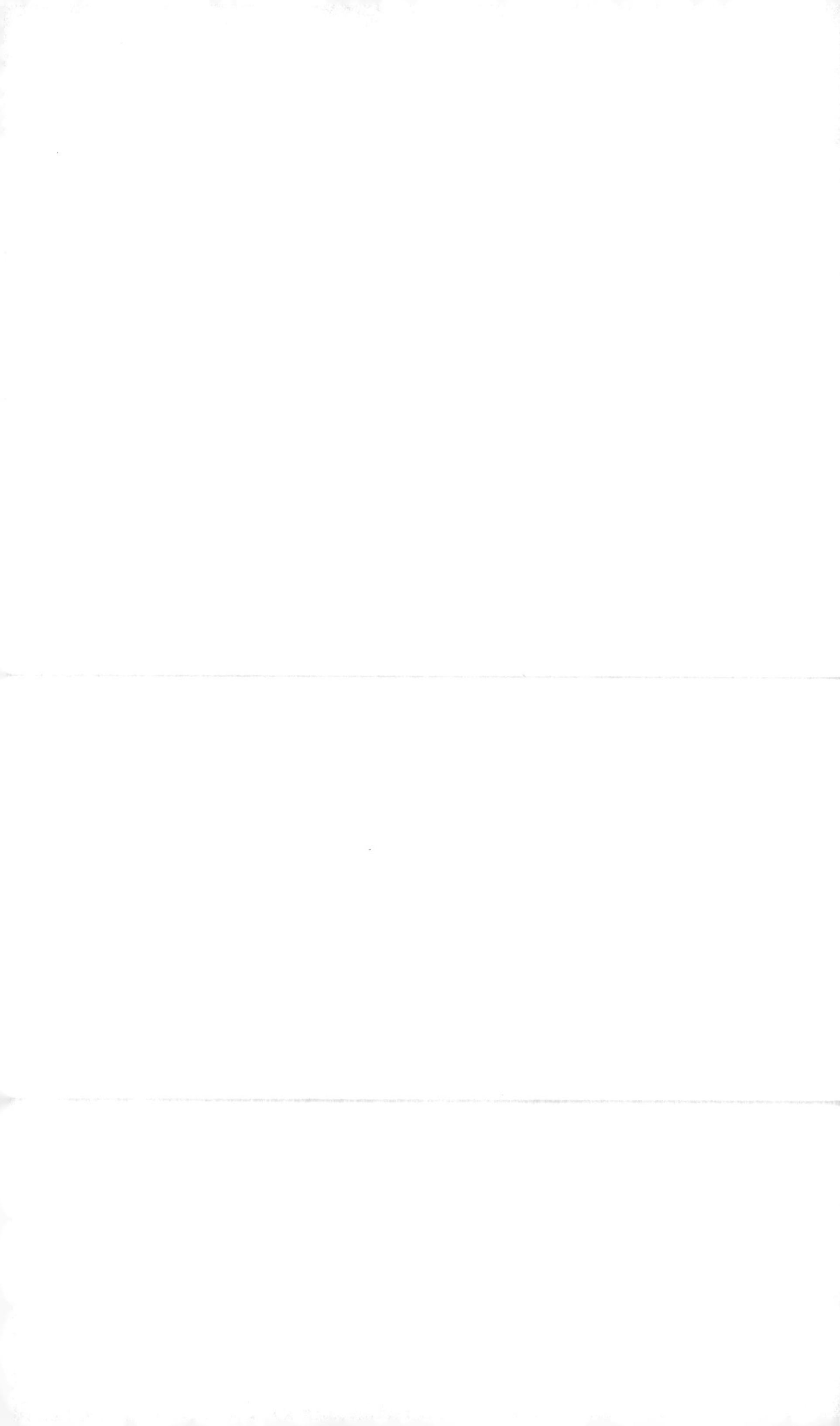

1

1868

MARTYN VAN DYKE CLUTCHED HIS LEATHER SATCHEL tightly and made sure the shoulder strap was secure. He didn't like being solely responsible for the sale of his family's cattle. At the age of twenty-five, not one thing he knew about Chicago or its stockyards made him want to travel there, especially alone. After loading the cattle on the train, he walked over to his mother to say goodbye.

"Martyn, I pray this will keep you safe. Bring it back to me." She pressed a small envelope into his hand, which he folded, shoved into his shirt pocket, and secured by buttoning the pocket flap.

She didn't have to say it. Of her four sons, Martyn knew he was her favorite. They were cut from the same cloth. She understood his love of learning and his desire to be a lawyer rather than a farmer. Before climbing aboard the train, he turned to wave to his parents. His father, Pieter, once tall and strong, now looked gaunt. After contracting dysentery during the Civil War, he'd returned home a compromised man.

Martyn wished his oldest brother Jan could have accompanied him to Chicago, but he already shouldered too many responsibilities for the farm. His second brother Dirk could once have managed the trip but, after accidentally killing his best friend in a hunting accident, he'd never been the same. He was now unstable, sometimes mean, often angry. His youngest brother Willem, at age twelve, was too young to help. That left Martyn, the best one with numbers, to take the cattle to market by himself.

The train pulled out on a warm June evening, scheduled to arrive at Chicago's Union Stock Yards the following morning. The Chicago, Iowa and Nebraska Railroad stretched across southern Iowa, a direct route to Chicago from their farm near the town of Pella. Settled by immigrants, small towns like this railroad stop straddled the lower tier of Iowa.

Martyn's parents' motivation for coming to America in 1848 was their desire to own land. When they first arrived in Pella, his father made furniture. When they weren't in school, his older brothers worked at the nearby river ferry. The family finally saved enough for the down payment on a farm but didn't have sufficient funds to buy it outright. This cattle sale would make that possible.

After darkness descended, Martyn slipped into reverie. When he was about to finish ninth grade, Martyn's father told him he needed him to work full-time on the farm. Immensely disappointed, Martyn couldn't sleep that night. After school the next day, he waited for the other students to leave and then approached his favorite teacher.

"Mr. DeJong, I'd like your advice about something. My father has decided I must quit school. He needs me on the farm."

"I'm sorry to hear that. You're my best student."

"Is there some way I could continue to study with you?"

"Yes, I think there is. I'll supply you with textbooks, and you may study at home. When you finish a subject, I'll test you to make sure you understand the material and then move you ahead to the next level. You're bright enough to do this."

"Thank you. I appreciate your willingness to help me."

"Is there something else you'd rather do than work the land?"

"Yes. Ever since I could read, I've had my nose stuck in a book. I want to read the law so I can be a lawyer."

"That's quite a goal. I have no doubt you can do it. I'm just curious as to how you arrived at that decision."

"Five years ago, my father and I went into town because he needed some documents notarized. It was my first time inside a law office. I was taken with the idea that someone, after reading the law, could make a livelihood representing and guiding clients on all sorts of issues."

"I could see you doing that. I wish you the best of luck. Also, I just received a new dictionary that I'd ordered for the classroom. You may have my old one. It's quite worn, but it still works." Mr. DeJong smiled at him.

Ever since that conversation, after chores and supper were finished, Martyn studied near the fireplace long after the others were asleep. He completed secondary school at seventeen, more determined than ever to study the law.

So today, after fulfilling his father's dream of owning land, Martyn could now pursue his own dream. He stared out the window at passing fields and dreamed about working in a law office. As soon as he returned from Chicago, he planned to order the first book of Henry John Stephen's *New Commentaries on the Laws of England*. There were four volumes he needed to read before he could seek an apprenticeship with an experienced lawyer. He intended to devour them as quickly as possible. That was how Abraham Lincoln became a lawyer. Martyn also knew he didn't want to practice law in their small town. The community was too stifling and judgmental. He felt sure his mother had an inkling of this but no one else in his family did.

The lumbering train rocked him to sleep across the Iowa prairie. When the train pulled into Chicago the next morning, the stench of Union Stock Yard and the meatpacking plants assaulted him. Union Stock Yard was thousands of times bigger than their feedlot. The need to feed Union troops during the Civil War had fed most of that expansion. The scope of the operation, with its massive number of livestock pens, meat-packing plants, and butchers, made him feel claustrophobic. Accustomed to the open prairie, the intensity of the operation unsettled him. Taking deep breaths to slow his racing pulse, he forced himself to calm down.

The sales transaction took place quickly. The cattle were transferred from the receiving area to holding pens and weighed. After that, Martyn met with the buying agent to agree on the price per pound, then went to the cashier and secured the bill of sale and payment in his inner jacket pocket. He was surprised at the efficiency of the transaction and relieved he could take the evening train home.

After stopping for a midafternoon dinner, he searched for a horse-drawn cart to take him to the train station. Not finding one, he started walking in what he believed was the right direction. There were a number of saloons and small hotels he didn't remember seeing before. After a couple of blocks, he realized he should have taken a turn down a previous street. When he turned around, the hair rose across the back of his neck. Two men were heading straight toward him. He'd seen one of them standing outside the cashier's office at the stock-yards.

Martyn pivoted and broke into a run to reach the cross street, hoping to find a policeman, anyone, to help him. When he left the train that morning, the station master had warned him to keep up his guard in Chicago. He said it was a rough city, that sometimes people just disappeared.

Martyn could usually run at a good pace, but his satchel slowed him down. He heard the men closing in on him. When they tackled him, he hit the ground hard. One man held him down while the other slammed his fist across Martyn's face. They both pulled at his satchel. Martyn tried to yell but was struggling to breathe. He wondered if this was how he was going to die. Then he heard a gunshot.

The next thing Martyn knew, an older man was bent over him. "Don't move. You have a bad cut near your eye. I'm pressing my handkerchief against it. The men ran away as soon as I fired my Colt."

Martyn slowly moved his right hand to feel for the payment documents. The inner pocket of his jacket was ripped open and empty. The man helped him sit up. Martyn checked to make sure his money belt was still under his shirt. He felt some relief knowing at least his personal cash was intact.

"Keep pressing this against your face. It'll stop the bleeding. Let me help you into my wagon. This city gets more lawless every day. I aimed for one of those thieves but missed. I am dog-tired of seeing these things. Did they take anything?"

"They took the payment for my family's cattle. I was heading to the railroad station."

"Let me look at that cut. I think he used brass knuckles on you, but it's not as deep as I feared. You'll likely bear a scar from this. Do you think you can ride a train tonight?"

Martyn nodded. "I need the Chicago, Iowa and Nebraska Railroad line. Could you please take me there?"

"Yes, I'm glad to do that. Do you already have a ticket?"

"No."

"You could save yourself some money if you find an empty boxcar and just climb into it. Most of the empty railroad cars are heading back to Wyoming for more cattle. If you decide to do that, you should be safe. If anyone is in the car, just stay in your own corner."

When they neared the rail yard, Martyn climbed down from the wagon with great care. The pain in his head affected his stability. "Thank you for rescuing me. I'm sure they intended to kill me. I wish I could repay you in some way."

"There's no need to worry about that, young man. I only wish I'd come by a few minutes sooner. I wish you good luck."

Martyn climbed into a boxcar at dusk. He assumed the car was empty but then saw a man hunched in one of the corners. The man nodded. Martyn returned the nod and sat down in the opposite corner of the car. He continued to press the handkerchief against the wound to staunch the bleeding. The pain made thinking difficult, but he had to make some decisions immediately.

His heart was beating fast because of the assault and also because he knew returning home was impossible. Martyn had no doubt his deranged brother would kill him, bringing further shame to their family. Two years ago, his brother had accidentally killed his best friend in a hunting accident. What made it even worse was that they had been hunting on Sunday, the Lord's Day. After that, some people in their church shunned his family. Martyn's disappearance and the loss of the farm would be regarded as further signs that God regarded the family with disfavor. His father and mother didn't subscribe to Reverend Scholten's strict religious philosophy, but many in the community did. Their god was a harsh god.

Martyn was shaking inside. No wonder his mother had given him her pendant. She was concerned something might happen. He'd felt it too—the sense that something might go wrong. He tried to slow his heart rate so he could think clearly. When he was ten years old, his mother had told him about prescience, the ability to sense something before it comes to pass. "You are the only one of my sons who possesses this. Your grandmother had this ability, and so do I. Be mindful of the images and feelings you receive. It's a different form of knowledge."

By disappearing and never returning home, whatever happened would remain an open-ended question for his family and the community. For all they knew, he could have been robbed and killed. Some might think he ran off with the money from the sale, but there would be no proof of that. His disappearance would cast a shadow over the family, but no one would ever really know what happened.

Martyn vowed to repay every cent that was stolen, no

matter how long it took. By then the family farm would probably be long gone, but keeping that promise was the only way he could live with himself. To keep from being traced, he'd have to change his name. He needed to lie his way to a new existence. How could this all be happening—his life upended within a matter of hours?

He made a quick assessment of his skills. As for making a living, he was better at working with cattle than with raising crops. He was good at it and liked it. He knew how to keep cattle healthy and get them ready for market. Also, he was a good hunter, on horse or on foot. He could set traps and track many creatures, especially those that killed cattle. He could shoot a rifle with a dead eye.

Because of the immense need to feed soldiers, the Civil War had spurred the development of cattle ranches in the newly formed Territory of Wyoming. He remembered reading that the Union Pacific Railroad had created a supply depot in the Dakota Territory a year ago and named it Cheyenne for the Cheyenne Indians who ranged there. Now, just a year later, the depot had expanded into a bustling small town.

His best bet would be to work on a ranch near Cheyenne. His woodworking ability was another asset he could bring to a ranching operation. When they began homesteading the farm, Martyn and his brothers worked alongside his father to construct the barn, outbuildings, corrals, and fences. He could do the same thing on a ranch. He needed to travel west, far beyond Iowa.

Before the train crossed the Illinois state line into Iowa, a horrific scent filled the car. It was worse than the stockyards. Martyn got up, walked to the middle of the railroad car, and pushed open the door a couple of feet. The distant air was murky with smoke. "What in tarnation caused this?"

"That's the smell of burning flesh." The man in the corner stood up and walked over to Martyn. "When people die from cholera, families cannot bury their loved ones. They have to burn them to keep the disease from spreading. When I passed through Indiana last month, I heard one town burned more than three hundred bodies."

Martyn could usually sense whether an individual was well-intentioned or whether he should have nothing to do with them. Sometimes he had visions about something that was going to happen. The old man in Chicago had warned him about talking to strangers on trains, but Martyn detected nothing threatening in the man's voice. He decided to trust him. "Thank you for explaining what happened. I have some biscuits and sausage in my satchel. Would you like some?"

The man nodded. "Thank you. I'd appreciate it."

They both sat down near the open door. The sausage and biscuits were wrapped inside an old flour bag. When Martyn pulled them out, he noticed a small envelope underneath them. He decided to look at it later. After dividing the food, he asked, "Do you know how far west this train is going?"

"It's heading to Wyoming to get more cattle. I'm getting off at Cheyenne. A year ago it was just a supply station for Union Pacific, but this year the Union Pacific directors selected Cheyenne as the location for a major depot and repair shop operation. Now, because of the construction gangs, it has a bustling merchant community. Of course, as with most boom towns, it has its share of bars, gamblers, and prostitutes."

Martyn noticed the man kept his hand over a small leather bag. He wondered what the man was protecting.

"This is my tool bag. I carry whetstones and an adze in it. Those tools have kept me alive. When I pass through a town, I can always make money sharpening knives and tools for people. I hope to find work in Cheyenne, but I could work on a ranch if I have to. Chicago was too rough a place for me to stay. How far west are you traveling?"

The man pronounced his words in softer tones than Martyn was accustomed to. There was nothing clipped about his speech. He wondered where the man was from. Perhaps from the South. Maybe he was one of those Confederate soldiers who returned home after the war and found there was nothing left for him to return to.

"I'm hoping to find work somewhere in the west. The truth is I went to Chicago to sell my family's cattle, which I did, but I was robbed on my way back to the train. I can't return home without the money. I need to find a way to repay the loss. As it stands, I'm just leaving the family farm sooner than I'd expected to. Our farm isn't big enough for four brothers to make a living from it."

The man nodded his head in acceptance and Martyn realized he was probably as concerned about making a livelihood as Martyn was.

"When the train stops in Council Bluffs, we'll have several hours before the ferry leaves for Omaha. It'll take years before they build a bridge across the Missouri River between Council Bluffs and Omaha. I hope to make some money sharpening tools when we stop. If you'd like to meet again, I'll be down at the ferry landing."

"Thank you. I'd like to do that. I feel safer traveling with you. I'm going to rest for a while."

Martyn returned to his side of the car, sat down, and sipped some water from his canteen. He felt exhausted, both mentally and physically. He leaned back into the corner but, before sleep enveloped him, he pulled out the little envelope from the flour bag. His mother had left a note for him. Moonlight flashing through the boxcar slats provided enough light for him to read. Also enclosed in the envelope was his grandmother's amber pendant.

Martyn, my heart is heavy with concern that you're traveling to Chicago by yourself. I will not be at peace until you return home. I pray Oma Magdalena's pendant will protect you. Bring this back to me, my beloved son. I asked your father to let Jan travel

*with you, but he said he needed him on the farm. I will not be
at peace until you return home. Bring this back to me, Martyn.*
   Your mother,
   Nell

Martyn knew how much the amber pendant meant to
his mother. His grandmother had given it to her just before
his family boarded the ship to America in 1853, both knowing they'd never see each other again. Five years old at the
time, Martyn still remembered his mother sobbing as the ship
pulled away, waving to her mother.

Tears stung his eyes. So his mother had also sensed something might go wrong. He needed to find a safe place for the
brooch and keep it near him, a talisman for his protection.
One day it might lead him back to her. He put her note and
the pendant in his shirt pocket, then he drifted off, sleeping
deeply until a dream forced him awake. In the dream, an old
woman was sitting near a fireplace, knitting. She turned to
look at him and said, "My name is Magdalena Handschuh."

In an instant he realized he needed to change his name. If
his parents reported him as missing, officials would be checking trains and towns for a young man named Martyn Van
Dyke. If he assumed a different name, it would be more difficult for him to be traced. His maternal grandmother's maiden
name was Handschuh, literally meaning "a shoe for the hand;
a glove." He assumed her ancestors came from a family of
glove makers. From now on, he decided, his last name would
be Handschuh, except he'd change the spelling of both names.
He would assume the name of Martin Handshoe, with the hope
that no one could trace him. Perhaps he could pass for someone of English descent. Martyn Van Dyke no longer existed.

Before he left, his mother had warned him about workers
traveling on trains. She was concerned they might threaten
him in some way. He first noticed them after the Civil War
ended. The man on the other side of the car didn't seem

threatening in any way. Martin decided to talk to him again before they got off the train. He got up and walked back across the car.

"I heard that train crews can be hostile to travelers like us. Do you have any advice?"

"Well, I expect Council Bluffs is far less dangerous than Chicago, but you still need to be careful. When the train stops, we need to get off quickly and walk away as if we were just passing by. I'm going to approach shop owners about sharpening tools and knives. If that doesn't work, I'll walk through town and ask homeowners about sharpening their knives and scissors. I'm not sure what you plan to do, but make sure to be polite. Say 'Ma'am' when you talk to the ladies."

"I'll make sure to do that. I don't have any tools but I could do odd jobs for a couple of hours. I'll meet you at the ferry landing. My name is Martin Handshoe." He extended his hand.

"And mine is James Connors." He shook Martin's hand

Martin headed to the business district. Small shops lined the main street, stretching for maybe half a mile. He saw James walk into a stable down the street. Without any tools, Martin's only option was physically working for food. The owner of the first café he approached looked at the gash on Martin's face and gruffly turned him away.

He noticed another café farther down on the other side of the street. Stepping inside, he approached the woman at the cash register.

"Excuse me, ma'am. Is the owner here?"

"I'm the owner. Could I help you with something?"

Martin was reluctant to remove his hat because of the wound but quickly doffed his hat to the woman. "I'm only here for several hours before the ferry leaves. I was wondering if I could work for some food. I'm good at repairing things. I could also chop wood or wash dishes. I'm willing to do anything that needs doing."

"Just go back out the front door and walk around to the back side of the café. I'll meet you there."

Martin stood on the back porch and waited. A small alley ran behind the café. There was a well in the backyard of the shop. Maybe he could pump some water for the café. He wanted to fill his canteen but not before meeting with the owner.

The screen door screeched open. The woman appeared with ham and biscuits. "Young man, you look as if you had a run-in with someone. I have a feeling your mother doesn't know where you are, does she?"

"No, ma'am. Thank you for the food." He accepted the food and sat down on the back steps.

She sat down next to him. "Are you running from something bad?"

"Yes, I was robbed after I sold my family's cattle in Chicago. I can't return home empty-handed. I need to find a way to repay them. I'm heading to Wyoming with my friend to work cattle."

"My husband passed away a year ago. Here's one of his shirts. It should fit you. When you finish eating, wash your shirt in the tub near the well, then hang it over that bush. It will dry in no time."

"Thank you, ma'am. I'm sorry for your loss."

"Thank you. Use this cloth to clean that wound. I'll be back shortly. Don't leave before then."

Martin nodded, his mouth too full to speak. After she went inside, he saved half the food for James and devoured the rest. He gingerly cleaned the cut near his eye and then washed his shirt. In the time it took for her to return, his shirt was almost dry. He was tucking it in his satchel when she reappeared.

"I see the desperation in your eyes. You don't need to tell me your story. I'm doing this for your mother. If you were my son, I'd want someone to help him. Here is some salve for that wound and some hardtack and sausage for you and your friend. This should be enough to get you to Wyoming."

"I can't thank you enough, ma'am. Someday, when I see my mother again, I'll tell her about you. I will never forget your generosity."

Martin walked to the ferry landing, spotted James at the edge of the gathering crowd, and walked over to him. "Did you find any work?"

"Yes, I sharpened scissors and some tools in several stores. How did you fare?"

"I didn't find any work, but we have enough food to get us to Cheyenne. I asked the owner of a café if I could help with any odd jobs. After one look at my face, she took pity on me. She gave me salve for the cut, handed me one of her deceased husband's shirts, and filled this flour bag with food. I will never forget her kindness."

James nodded. "That is indeed an act of mercy. The horrors of the Civil War continue to haunt me. It's good to know there is still some decency in this world." He looked away and focused on the steamboat approaching the landing.

Martin wondered what horrific events James had witnessed. His father never discussed his service in the Civil War, but his memories haunted him after he returned home. Sometimes he cried out during the night. His nightmares were always about the war.

"I looked through my satchel and counted my money. I have enough for the ferry and for the train ticket from Omaha to Cheyenne. Or do you think we should ride in an empty freight car?"

James turned and looked at him, his mind returning from some distant place. "Even though we have enough money for tickets, I think we should climb into a boxcar just before the train leaves Omaha. After delivering cattle to the Chicago stockyards, almost all the freight cars will be empty. There's no need to waste our money. The train is scheduled to leave late afternoon."

Martin nodded in agreement. "I'm very thankful to be traveling with you."

"I feel the same. We're safer traveling as two rather than one."

When the steamboat opened its gates for boarding, Martin and James were among the first to step aboard. They made their way to one of the side rails and watched the boarding proceed.

"I'd like to sit on the port side of the ferry. I want to watch the Missouri rolling south to St. Louis." James pointed in the direction of some benches.

Martin looked at James and nodded. "That's fine with me. It'll be good to sit for a while."

"The river seems roiled. I wonder if there were storms on the High Plains."

"That's quite possible. Summer storms can strike quickly and with a vengeance. Are you concerned about the river current, James?"

"No. This is just a new experience for me. I'll be relieved when we reach Omaha and locate the train station. We should be well on our way to Wyoming by nightfall."

At that moment the steamboat horn blared.

"We're leaving on time. That's a relief. I've never done anything quite like this. Truth be told, I'm more than a bit nervous." James tapped his fingers against his tool bag.

James's statement surprised Martin. There was a certain reserve about him, which Martin had taken for self-confidence. He now realized James was also concerned about entering uncharted waters. Whatever circumstances lay ahead for them, he was grateful to be traveling with him. "I don't know much about the Territory of Wyoming except that the Union Pacific crosses it heading northwest. What made you decide to go to Cheyenne?"

James leaned against the railing, looking west as if to find sight of Omaha. "Surely you're aware of the massive devastation that exists across the South. After the war, when many

Confederate soldiers returned to their cities and farms, their homes and land lay in ruin. Making a livelihood was difficult. And for those who depended upon slavery, impossible. My family did not hold slaves.

"I never supported slavery. I fought for the North, but my older brother fought for the Confederacy. Our family land is in southern Missouri. When I came home after the war, my brother made it clear I wasn't welcome. He told me to leave, that he didn't want to see me ever again. He refused to let me enter our family home to see my mother. My father died during the war and my brother is now the head of the family. My mother couldn't make him see things differently. I had no choice but to leave immediately."

"Did you expect he might feel this way?"

"I didn't know what to expect. I knew he was upset with me for not siding with the Confederacy. I can't begin to describe how horrible conditions were during the war and afterwards. Every man who fought in the war came back a changed person. You were fortunate not to have to witness it."

"I'm sorry this happened to you. My father served briefly in the war. He contracted dysentery shortly after he was drafted and never regained his strength. When he returned home, we barely recognized him, but at least our family remained together."

"When my brother slammed the front door in my face, I turned around and walked away as if leaving the farm. But then I circled back, went to the barn, and gathered the tools I carry in my satchel—a whetstone, an awl, and a small adze. It was all I could carry with ease. My mechanical skills far exceed those of my brother. With the proper tools and my skills, I felt sure I could make a living.

"First I went to St. Louis, but I had difficulty making enough money to live on. After that I moved to Chicago. It was more lucrative but also more dangerous. I never felt safe. When I heard talk about a growing cattle town called

Cheyenne, I decided to head west. It will be the capital of the Territory of Wyoming, and it's a major depot for the Union Pacific Railroad. I should be able to find work quickly. Also, Cheyenne has become a major shipping point for sending cattle to the east. Are you aware of the cattle drives heading north out of Texas?"

Martin shook his head. "I know very little about it. Nothing in any detail."

"Texans are driving large herds north. Besides cattle being shipped east, the Union Pacific Railroad needs them to feed its crews. Government forts and outposts also need livestock. This business is growing at a fast pace. Even some European companies are investing in ranches there.

"Because of the devastation in the South, many Confederate soldiers never returned home. One way or another, a lot of them are involved in the cattle business. Some of them are driving cattle from Texas to Wyoming and then staying there. Martin, I need to rest for a bit. I'll keep my hands on my belongings, but please watch over me. I'll do the same for you after I rest."

"Of course, I'll do that. Once we climb aboard the train, I plan to sleep for a long time."

2

MARTIN PUT A HAND OVER HIS BAG AND A HAND BESIDE
James's bag. He mulled over James's comments about Wyoming's
cattle ranches. The cattle business was something Martin
understood. He could also work in a store. Thanks to his
secondary teacher, his mathematics and writing skills were
strong. James had advised him that, while it was important to
seem confident of one's skills, laying them out too forcefully
could prevent someone from hiring him.

Because his preference was to work on a ranch, Martin
started mentally compiling reasons why a rancher should
hire him. Besides cattle, Martin knew a lot about breaking in
horses. His father had once accepted a horse in payment for
money loaned to a friend. The horse had never been properly
broken. It was ornery and bordered on mean. When Martin
found marks on the horse, he was sure the former owner had
abused it. Once he understood that, he was determined to heal
the horse.

Every day, Martin put a lead on the horse, walked it to a
small pasture, and set the horse free. He pretended to ignore
it while he cut some prairie grass and made a pile of the cut-
tings. The horse eventually came over and ate the grass. Each
day Martin moved the pile of grass closer to himself, and the
horse eventually came to trust him. By the end of the summer,
Martin was able to ride him.

While he didn't want to earn his living as a carpenter, that was also a possibility. His grandfather in the Netherlands made quality furniture and had passed that trade on to Martin's father. In turn, he taught this skill to his sons. Martin had never attained his father's skill level, but he could make functional furniture. His father's sturdy fences were some of the best in their township, a skill Martin did acquire.

He could dowse for water. Mr. Van Etten, an older Dutchman in their community, was quite successful at finding water on settlers' farms. When he came to their homestead to search for water, Martin begged to be allowed to spend the day with him. His father, eldest brother, and Martin went out on horseback with the dowser. Periodically the old man halted his horse and walked around, holding a forked willow branch with both hands facing down. Finally, late in the afternoon, the divining rod drew Mr. Van Etten's hands down toward the soil. When they dug a trench the next day, they found a spring not far from their house.

After that outing, Martin wanted to learn more about dowsing and asked Mr. Van Etten if he could accompany him sometime. The old gentleman said he'd welcome Martin's company any time. His father agreed to it but insisted Martin's chores on the farm had to come first. When they rode through fields, Mr. Van Etten pointed out terrain features that could indicate a water source. Martin carried a small notebook with him and took notes about everything he was learning.

One day, Martin was carrying the willow branch for Mr. Van Etten when he felt the stick twitch. The old gentleman noticed it.

"Martin, please hand me the branch."

When Mr. Van Etten took hold of the willow branch, it moved in his hands. "I'm sure there is a water source here. I can't explain how this occurs. Most people don't succeed with using a divining rod, but I believe you have a talent for dowsing. It's a gift. I'll give you one of my divining rods."

From then on, Mr. Van Etten paid Martin to work with him

when he needed assistance. As long as Martin did his share of the farm work, his father agreed to it. Martin knew his father was proud of his talent for dowsing but would never admit it. His words of praise were few and far between. He didn't want Martin to become arrogant.

On a summer afternoon when they were dowsing, Mr. Van Etten said, "I need to sit down for a while. Those boulders along the creek bank will make a good resting place." After they sat down, the dowser started reminiscing.

"My family came from a small village in Flanders. Before we moved to America, my mother sometimes consulted an old woman who sought answers by dowsing with a crystal. This is not related to searching for water. It is a method to gain clarity about a specific situation. My mother was very secretive about this because Father did not believe in it."

Martin was immediately curious. "Do you ever use a crystal to find something or to seek an answer to a question?"

Mr. Van Etten smiled. "I tried it once or twice but wasn't successful. Dowsing for water is what I'm meant to do."

Martin was fascinated with the concept of consulting a crystal for guidance. He searched the creek bed on their property for crystals but had no luck. Then, several months later, he and his younger brother were fishing in the river when Martin spied a piece of quartz. The next time he saw Mr. Van Etten, he showed him the crystal.

"Well, it's a bit cloudy, but it might work. I just happen to have some string in my pocket. I'll tie it around the crystal and show you how it works. Hold the string gently between your thumb and index finger, like this. Just let it hang. Now, a pendulum may swing in different directions. It can swing clockwise, counterclockwise, backward, forward, side-to-side.

"Each time you use it, you'll have to determine exactly how it's swinging on that given day. Ask it a question you know the answer to so you can determine how it's swinging. This is not a toy. It can also be used to assess people. You must treat it with respect."

"Thank you, Mr. Van Etten. I know you have to work today, but sometime may I try this when I'm with you?"

"Of course. It pleases me that you're interested in mysterious things."

"What do you mean by using the crystal to assess people?"

"You're blessed with a strong sense of intuition, but here's an example of how you could use the crystal. Let's say someone new shows up in town. The first time he approaches you, you think he seems a bit forward. If something about this person doesn't seem right, this is where you could consult the crystal.

"When you're alone, determine which way the crystal is swinging that day. Then ask if it's safe to meet with this person. I'm not a crazy old man. If you ever have misgivings about a situation, you could do this. Are you familiar with the word 'premonition'?"

Martin nodded his head. "Yes, sometimes my mind warns me about things."

"I suspected this. Do you also have visions?"

"I often sense when storms are coming before we can see them. Is that what you mean?"

"No. We'll talk about visions later. They're another form of knowledge."

Martin regretted that they never explored the concept of visions. Then he realized the dream about his grandmother on the train was a vision. As soon as his grandmother said, "My name is Magdalena Handschuh," Martin had realized he had to change his family name to prevent being traced.

Martin stopped his reverie and thought about the attack in Chicago. Thanks to the intervention of the old gentleman, he was still alive. Was that an accident or was there a larger force at work? What about his climbing into what he assumed was an empty boxcar and then meeting James? Was there such a thing as destiny?

With Omaha now in sight, some passengers lined the ship railing while others were queueing to leave the steamboat. Martin looked over at James, who was waking up.

"I feel much better now. Thank you for watching my bag. Let's head to the lower level. I don't want to be one of the last ones leaving the boat."

"I agree."

They shouldered their possessions and headed toward the exit.

James assessed the number of people heading to the Union Pacific station. "The station is closer to the ferry landing than I thought it would be. Let's let anyone heading to the passenger cars get ahead of us. When we find an empty cattle car near the rear of the train, we'll climb into it."

"That shouldn't be a problem. I can see some open cattle cars from here." Relief raced through Martin.

Within half an hour, they'd climbed into a boxcar and closed the doors. After the train started moving, Martin reached into his satchel and pulled out the food the café owner had given him.

"James, I'll divide the food now so you may decide when you want to eat. I'm exhausted and want to be rested when we reach Cheyenne. I'm going to eat soon. It'll be dark before long."

"I'll eat when you do. I've been thinking about what will happen once we arrive in Cheyenne. Before we separate to look for work, let's find a place to meet later in the day. We'll need to find a place to sleep, and I want to talk about how the day went."

"That sounds good. We'll both know a lot more by tomorrow evening."

After eating they went to separate corners, settled against their small bags, and let the train's motion rock them to sleep.

Martin woke up several times, glanced at the changing landscape, then let the train's motion lull him back to sleep.

In the middle of the night, the train slowed for a curve and woke Martin. He'd been dreaming about leaving the farm and reading the law. Neither one of those was happening the way he'd anticipated.

Just before sunrise, a change in the train's sound woke Martin again. The engine seemed to be working harder. The air felt cooler, drier. When James stirred, Martin walked over to him.

"We must be at a higher altitude. The air feels thinner."

"Yes. It definitely feels different." James looked at his pocket watch. "We should arrive in Cheyenne in about two hours. I saw a map of the town before I left Chicago. Main Street lies a couple of blocks north of the train station."

"I've been awake for a while, trying to slow my racing mind. After we decide where to meet later today, I'll head to the stockyards. I don't want to meet in a bar. My family was very strict about not drinking alcohol, and I prefer to keep it that way. I don't want to be around any belligerent drunks. I already look as if I just came from a fight."

"I understand, Martin. I agree with you about bars. After we leave the train, walk with me to the main street so we can decide where to meet later. God willing, we'll both find some kind of work."

They jumped from the train as soon as it drew to a stop and headed into town. When they got to the main street, Martin noticed a small café next to a bank. "Let's see how late that café stays open. It looks like a good place to meet."

"The sign says it's open until eight o'clock. How about meeting here at five o'clock? After we eat, we can decide where to spend the night."

"That sounds good. I wish you the best of luck."

"I wish you the same, Martin."

When Martin reached the stockyard, crews were preparing to load cattle into boxcars that would leave late that afternoon for the Chicago stockyards. He walked through the crowd, asking about ranches that needed hired hands. Someone pointed out the right-hand man for a rancher who was loading cattle on the train. Martin watched him closely. The cowboy was making sure the cattle were properly loaded and was staying there until that was done.

When the man finally turned away from the train, Martin approached him. "I just arrived on this morning's train. I'm looking for work as a ranch hand and heard your ranch might need some help."

The ranch hand eyed him over. "Where are your cowboy boots?"

"These work boots suit me just fine. They've seen me through many rough conditions and have held up well."

"Have you been in a fight?" The ranch hand spoke tersely. "Where did you get that cut near your eye? I don't want any troublemakers."

"Someone tried to rob me at a train stop in Nebraska. I fought him off, but he did a little damage."

"It looks as if you didn't protect yourself very well."

"Well, you should have seen how he looked when I finished with him." For someone who tried to never break the Ten Commandments, Martin was surprised at how easily lying came to him. Then he decided it was not so much lying as being evasive.

The ranch hand chuckled. "What kind of work can you do?"

"I grew up on a farm and worked with overseeing our cattle. My brothers were more involved with raising crops. I helped with planting and harvesting, but I was mostly responsible for the cattle. I made sure they had the right kind of feed, moved them around to different pastures, and watched them closely for any signs of disease. Treating them early makes all the difference. Our cattle were healthy. I shoed our horses and also helped break horses. Also, I can dowse for water. I did that on my family farm and other farms in the community."

"Well, I'll give you a chance to prove yourself. The owner of the ranch is Doc Matheson. Everyone calls him Doc because he's an expert when it comes to raising cattle. He came to Cheyenne about eighteen months ago. He and four cowboys drove a herd of longhorns here from Texas. Two of the cowboys went back. I am one of the two who remained here with him.

"The ranch he started was small, but he has gradually acquired more land. Also, the ranch is surrounded by public range so there's plenty of land for grazing. He knows how to handle cattle and how to treat the men who work for him. I have some things to take care of today and will head back to the ranch tomorrow. Meet me here at eight o'clock tomorrow morning."

"Yes, sir. I'll be here. I promise you will not regret hiring me. My name is Martin Handshoe."

"And mine is Jake Wilson. I need to get back to work. I'll see you in the morning."

Wilson extended his hand. When they shook hands, relief coursed through Martin. He sensed Wilson would give him a chance to prove himself. At least for now, he was going to be all right in his new world. A sense of calm came over him.

Late in the afternoon, when Martin headed to the café, he saw James coming down the street. He looked serious but confident.

"Martin, I'm paying for your dinner. After trying to find work at several stores, I went into McGrady's General Store and convinced Mr. McGrady to give me a two-week trial period. I start tomorrow. He seems to be a decent man. Also, I think this was an auspicious day for us to arrive in Cheyenne. Today President Andrew Johnson officially established the Territory of Wyoming. It was carved from the Dakota, Idaho, and Utah

Territories. There are already four thousand people living here."

"All of that sounds good. I have some good news too. The boss man for a cattle ranch is willing to give me a chance to prove myself. The ranch owner is Doc Matheson, just in case you ever hear any reference to him. The man who hired me said Doc Matheson knows how to handle cattle and how to treat the men who work for him. All I need is a chance to prove myself."

"Let's have dinner and figure out where we can spend the night. I noticed a stable on one of the back streets. Maybe we could sleep in the hayloft above it. What do you think?"

"I like that idea. I have more than enough money if the caretaker decides to charge us for a night's stay. I need to be at the stockyard early tomorrow morning. Let's take our time having supper. I'd just like to sit and talk for a while."

Before leaving the café a couple of hours later, James bought some biscuits. "These will get us off on the right foot tomorrow."

After they were settled in the hayloft, Martin decided to be completely honest with James about his decision to flee west. "James, I know this isn't necessary, but I'd like to further explain why I decided not to return home. I'm the third of four sons. My second brother has been crazed ever since he accidentally killed his best friend in a hunting accident. I have no doubt he would have killed me if I'd returned home without any money from the sale of our cattle. And that would have brought incredible shame upon my family. The church my family attends judges people harshly. So now, even though I can't prevent my family from losing their farm, I'll be able to make restitution to them, which I couldn't do from a grave. Also, I changed my family name to Handshoe to prevent anyone from tracing me."

"Ah, so you also have a hateful brother. Yet another thing we share. I also changed my family name. I appreciate your honesty. I'm exhausted, and I expect you are too. Since we've both left our families, perhaps we can become like brothers, even though you speak with a slightly different accent."

"I mostly spoke Dutch with my father, and I think that somewhat affected my pronunciation of English. I'll work on my accent. Within a couple of months, I aim to have an acceptable Western accent." Before he fell asleep, Martin gave thanks for the presence of James in his life. He seemed to be heaven-sent.

Just before daybreak, Martin walked over to James. "I'm sorry to wake you, but I'm going to leave now. Thank you for dinner and for the biscuits. I hope to see you before long."

"I look forward to that. Good luck."

After washing down the biscuits with a cup of coffee, Martin headed to the stockyard, making sure he arrived before Jake Wilson. He draped his arms over the stockyard fence and watched his new world come to life.

"Good morning, Mr. Wilson."

"And good morning to you. Mr. Wilson's too formal. Most folks call me Jake. That buckboard wagon belongs to the ranch. You can help me hitch up the horses. Have you ever worked with quarter horses?"

"No, sir. Where I grew up, farmers mostly used draft horses. But, from what I've read about quarter horses, they're perfect for the West. They're said to have a calm disposition and natural talent for working with cattle."

"That's correct. They have more cattle sense than any other type of horse I can think of."

"Who buys your cattle?"

"Mainly the Chicago packing houses, but, because of the track-laying crews, the Union Pacific Railroad is also a big cus-tomer."

After they left Cheyenne, the road became rough.

"Martin, I'm not much for small talk, so don't take it personally. I need to concentrate on getting to the ranch as soon as possible. See those thunderheads building on the horizon?"

Martin nodded. "Yes sir. I've been watching them. They look powerful."

"They are indeed. I want to get to the ranch before that storm breaks loose. We should be there within the hour."

Martin admired how Jake handled the quarter horses, guiding them around ruts, washouts, and prairie dog burrows. The horses exhibited a good combination of strength and intelligence in handling the rough surfaces. As for the landscape, Martin could see why they were driving cattle from Texas here. The rolling prairies of these High Plains looked to be a perfect place to raise them.

The wind started picking up, flinging grit at them. "Martin, that big log cabin is the ranch house. We keep this wagon under a lean-to near the barn. The stable's next to it. As soon as I pull up to the stable, take the horses inside. The bunkhouse is next to that. After I secure the wagon, I'll come to the stable. Then I'll take you to the bunkhouse, show you where your bed is, and introduce you to some of the cowboys. The cookhouse is just behind the bunkhouse. Everyone makes their own supper from what's available in the cookhouse."

When the cook rang the bell for noon dinner, Martin restrained himself from taking too much food. The cook served biscuits, beans, and stewed beef. Martin couldn't remember ever feeling this hungry. He ate a second helping after making sure the other cowhands had taken what they wanted. After the thunderstorm passed, Jake showed Martin around the stable and corrals and pointed out a horse they were having trouble training.

After he fixed himself supper, Martin listened to the bunkhouse conversation for a short time, then excused himself. Exhausted from the massive shift in his life, he tumbled into his assigned bed and sank into a deep sleep.

Deep in the night, his mother's face appeared to him through a haze. She was wondering where he was and why he hadn't returned home. She felt the amber talisman hadn't kept him safe. The vision was vivid and woke him up. Martin promised he'd let her know, when the time was right, that he was alive. He tried to slow the pace of his thoughts. He was physically and mentally exhausted and needed to be ready to work in a couple of hours.

Martin woke just before daybreak and quietly left the bunkhouse. He leaned against the corral fence and studied his new universe. Maybe it was the altitude, but the sky's expanse seemed boundless. He took a deep breath and bent his head in thanksgiving. He needed to create a new existence for himself from this moment on and eventually make restitution to his family. Self-pity reared its ugly head, and he squelched it.

From there he went to the kitchen shed to get breakfast, and Jake came in just after him. "Before I take you to camp out on the range, there's something I want you to tackle. We have a young quarter horse that was never properly broken. A former cowhand was rough with him. I want you to see if you can salvage him. If he proves impossible to train, I won't hold you accountable.

"He's a bit wild, but I hope we won't have to get rid of him. He's beautiful and smart. For the next week or two, you can work on the range, but return here around four o'clock in the afternoon to train him. I'll give you a week or two to see if you can make any progress with him."

"I welcome that challenge. I'll try everything I know."

"You can work with him this afternoon. Right now I have some other things for you to do."

Midafternoon, Jake took Martin to the paddock near the barn. "Well, here he is. He likes being around that older horse over there. When you're finished working with him, you can release him into that pasture so he can be with his buddy."

Martin wasn't familiar with quarter horses, but this was the most beautiful horse he'd ever set eyes on. Its face was handsome, and its burnished sorrel coat was striking. There was a distinguishing white mark running down his nose. Martin wanted this horse for himself.

"He's beautiful. I can see why you want to give him one more chance. I'll do my best. It might take time to train him, but I usually succeed."

"Well, I hope you can get him to cooperate. Let me know when you want me to take a look at him. You can spend mornings on the range and come back late each afternoon to work with him."

After Jake left, Martin climbed over the fence and walked midway into the enclosure, gathering some grasses along the way. He remembered his father had once accepted a horse as payment for a debt. The horse had been beaten and whipped. Knowing that Martin had a way with horses, his father asked him to see if he could train it. It took a while, but, after a couple of months, Martin was able to ride him and work him in the fields.

Remembering all this, Martin walked over to a large boulder in the pasture. Before sitting on it, he set the grasses down about six feet behind him. He noted where the horse was and then turned his back to it. After waiting patiently, Martin heard the horse chomping on the grasses. Gently, he said, "I'm not looking at you. You have nothing to fear. I want you to get used to the sound of my voice."

Martin continued in a stream of words, saying whatever came into his mind, always speaking in a gentle tone. When he no longer heard the horse eating, Martin turned around. It was back near the fence, looking at Martin.

Several days later, Martin extended his right arm and offered the horses some grass. Both horses took the grass and ate it where they stood, only a few feet from him. Martin looked directly at the young one. "I promise to take good care of you. I'll never harm you. That mark running down your nose looks like a lightning bolt. From now on I'll call you Blaze."

Blaze was close enough for Martin to see several areas of proud flesh on his shoulder, undoubtedly the result of being whipped. The wounds seemed to be healing well.

This routine continued late each afternoon, with Martin inching the grass bundle closer to himself each day. He always spoke in soothing tones. Sometimes the horse snorted in response.

After several days, Martin talked to Jake after supper. "I think it would be helpful if that old horse could be in the paddock when I work with Blaze."

"Blaze. So you've given him a name. As for the old horse, it's fine with me if he's in the paddock with you two."

Martin trained Blaze with great care, not wanting to push him too far in any session, and he always kept the old horse with them in the paddock. When he noticed any sign of anxiety like tail wringing or fear in Blaze's eyes, he immediately stopped the training and just let him graze. Martin's father always made sure their horses had grazing time. He said it was nature's way of lubricating their joints and keeping their feet healthy. After each session, he let Blaze and the old horse wander in the paddock and nibble grass. Sometimes he walked with them, keeping his distance, but other times he walked close beside Blaze.

Before returning Blaze to the pasture, Martin always groomed and gently massaged him, checking to make sure he wasn't in pain. If Blaze flinched, he gently worked the spot until the muscle tension eased. He sensed a bond developing between the two of them and expected to ride Blaze on the range before long. Within two weeks, Blaze whinnied when he saw Martin coming to get him. The first few times this happened, Martin blinked away tears. Having abandoned his family, he finally realized that building a relationship with this horse had probably taken on more significance than it should have. At any rate, he regarded Blaze as family and knew the bond was working both ways.

One evening, Martin stopped Jake outside the bunkhouse. "Do you have time to stop by tomorrow and watch me with Blaze? I think he's making good progress, but I'd like to know what you think."

"All right. I'll stop by tomorrow afternoon."

Late the next afternoon, Martin looked up and saw Jake leaning against the fence. Martin rode over to him, then set Blaze free to graze. "I just noticed you. How long have you been here?"

"Long enough to see that Blaze finally trusts someone. I'm glad we won't have to get rid of him. I expect you know this, but when horses like someone or feel pleased about something, their ears go forward. His ears just did that with you. I think he's ready to be out on the range. After breakfast tomorrow, let's head out there. Doc just gave me an old Winchester rifle for you. I'll give it to you tomorrow."

In mid-August, Jake and Martin rode out to the open range.

"You should always have a fairly good idea of where the chuck wagon is," Jake said. "Every few days Chef and his helper move the wagon to a new location, but never too great a distance from the last one. Until you get a feel for this, don't ride too far away from the mess wagon. You'll soon understand how to locate it. Also, just in case you can't make it back to camp, ride with your bedroll behind your saddle. If you stay out on the range, make sure you're near a water source. Horses need about ten gallons of water each day. Finding grass won't be a problem. Do you have any questions?"

Martin shook his head. "No questions right now."

When they reached camp and Jake showed him the mess wagon, Martin was impressed. It was loaded with a cook stove, a cook tent, and enough provisions to feed men for five to six weeks before restocking. The bed wagon contained bedrolls, horseshoes, rope, and tacking of all kinds.

"Chef makes a hearty breakfast at daybreak. The fare is meat, beans, bread, and strong black coffee. It'll keep you going most of the day. Always keep some hardtack and dried beef in your saddlebag, in case you can't make it back to the chuck wagon by day's end."

Martin liked being out on the range. Most nights he made it back to camp, but his blanket roll was always behind his saddle. He felt comfortable sleeping under the immense night sky surrounded by cattle. The freedom of the open range was a stark contrast to Iowa's farmland. With no fences to restrict them, cattle roamed the range in search of grasses and water. Cowboys went off by themselves, following cattle in every direction. Martin liked the challenge of rounding up strays and had a sixth sense of where they were likely to be found. He enjoyed the freedom of it all.

About a week later, Jake came riding up to him at camp. It was late afternoon and cowboys were riding in for supper. "I heard you're good at tracking down strays. How do you know where to look for them?"

"First of all, I look for tracks. Any kind of tracks. I want to know if there are predators or other grazing critters nearby. The other thing I watch for is any water source. Cattle and predators need water as much as we do. Sometimes I just have a hunch where they might be. When Blaze slows his pace and shakes his head, it usually means he senses some kind of predator. Because of their eye placement, horses can look in two directions at the same time. Between the two of us, Blaze and I can observe a lot of territory. I always let him set the pace when I scan the horizon for wild cats and stray cattle."

"Well, it seems to come more natural to you than it does to most of us."

Martin smiled and shrugged off the compliment. "Does Doc Matheson ever come out on the range?"

"Not very often. When we first came here, he spent a lot of time on the range. Now he works on trying to improve the breed of his stock. Last year he brought in some shorthorn bulls from Oregon to breed with his longhorns. He's always looking for a better way to do things."

Martin thought for a few seconds. "I think it also means he has a lot of confidence in his cowboys. He knows he can trust them to handle his cattle."

"The fall roundup will start in about a month. We hire extra hands for that. After we separate the two- and three-year-old steers from the herd, we drive them to town. From there, they'll be sent to the slaughterhouses in Chicago. I'll see you at the chuck wagon." Jake nodded and rode off.

3

AFTER RETURNING TO CAMP EACH NIGHT FOR A WEEK, Martin started ranging farther afield. During the day, he and Blaze roamed at an easy pace, checking on the locations of the cattle, some of them far-flung. Blaze took to it like it was second nature. Martin carried extra rations of dried beef, dried fruit, and sourdough bread in case they didn't make it back to camp. He also made sure they camped near water. Before falling asleep, he recorded his observations in a small journal, noting water sources, grazing conditions, and any predators he spotted.

When they were on the range, he encouraged Blaze to make bursts of speed. An old pioneer told him horses needed this to develop strong feet and bones. It was obvious Blaze liked those sessions. He was more intelligent than any horse Martin had ever known. When Martin wanted to isolate some of the ranch's cattle, Blaze read his mind. He moved carefully into the herd and easily separated the few head that Martin wanted.

The night sky mesmerized him. Martin wondered if it was the altitude that made the sky seem appreciably closer. Masses of brilliant stars blanketed the heavens. The nighttime cries of coyotes lulled him to sleep and birdsong awakened him before dawn. His new universe suited him.

One night, just as he was sinking into sleep, he felt a light pressure pass across his forehead. When he was a young boy, his mother did this when she tucked him into bed. He wanted to believe her spirit had found him, that she knew he was alive. Sometimes guilt lurked at the edge of his conscience, blaming him for the loss of the family farm. When this happened, Martin stifled it, vowing to make amends as soon as he possibly could. Dwelling on it wouldn't change anything.

In mid-September, Jake hired some extra cowboys to help with the fall roundup. Martin had never seen anything like this. Cowboys from various ranches rounded up the widely scattered cattle and then separated them by their brands. After that, each ranch separated the two- and three-year-old steers from their herd. Those steers would be sent by rail to Chicago.

After spending a week on the range, Martin returned to the ranch in early October. The following morning, Jake sat down next to him for breakfast. It was a beautiful fall morning with just a hint of winter's chill. The cookhouse door was wide open.

"I'm going to Cheyenne tomorrow to pick up some supplies," Jake said. "Want to keep me company?"

Martin nodded. "Yes. Thanks for asking. Let me know if I can help with anything."

"I will, but mostly you'll be on your own. We'll head back early Sunday morning. That'll give you a chance to have supper with your friend. Meet me at the stable tomorrow morning at seven-thirty."

"I'll be waiting for you."

When Martin entered the general store, James was ringing up a customer. "I've been wondering when I'd see you again. Are you staying in town tonight?"

"Yes. I came to town with Jake. We'll head back to the ranch early tomorrow morning."

"The room I rent is small but you're welcome to sleep

there. I could throw some blankets on the floor for you. I finish work at five o'clock so be back here by then. I know a good place to have supper. Also, I'd already invited an old frontiersman to have supper with me, so he'll be joining us. Zeke traveled out here in the late 1830s and made his living as a trapper. He knows a lot about the West."

Martin spent the rest of the day walking the streets of Cheyenne, making note of the number of law offices. He had to bide his time, but this looked like a good place to practice law. Right now, his main objective was to save enough money to order Henry John Stephen's *New Commentaries on the Laws of England.*

When James left the general store at five, Martin was outside waiting for him. "We're meeting Zeke at Ford Restaurant. It's just down the street. The food is good and so are the prices. So tell me about life on a cattle ranch. You look more relaxed and confident than the last time I saw you."

"The ranch is well-run. Doc Matheson, the owner, drove his cattle here from Texas last year. He knows how to manage a ranch and has a reputation for being fair with his ranch hands. Jake, the cowboy who hired me, has taken me under his wing. He's a patient man. Working on a ranch is very different from homesteading farmland. I've learned a lot from him and feel secure about keeping my job for now."

"I think Jake took you under his wing because he could tell you're a decent man and just needed a chance to prove yourself."

"You may be right. He gave me the opportunity to break in a difficult horse. A previous hired hand was abusive to the horse and made it extremely skittish. Jake said if I couldn't train it, they were going to sell him. He let me handle it my way, and now the horse is mine."

"Sounds like you and your horse both needed a chance to prove yourselves. You seem to have a strong attachment to that horse."

"I do. We've both survived difficult situations. He knows he can trust me, and I feel the same way about him."

"Now that's an interesting observation because a similar thing happened between the owner of the store and me. Frank McGrady, the owner, keeps increasing my responsibilities. He says his customers like me. When ladies pick up the scissors and knives they've left to be sharpened, they usually buy some other items. I don't push them, but I try to make sure they have everything they need. I believe Cheyenne will be a good place for me to plant roots."

"I agree with you. I'd like to practice law here."

"Before we get to the restaurant, there are a few things I want you to know about Zeke. He came out west in the 1830s with a friend and made his living as a trapper. You and I are not the only ones who had to flee from family. He left his family even earlier than we did. Although he no longer lives in the mountains, he's a mountain man at heart."

"I've never met a mountain man. This should be an interesting evening."

After James made introductions and they ordered supper, Martin started the conversation. "Zeke, it's good to make your acquaintance. James has told me a few things about you. If you don't mind, I'd like to hear your story about deciding to head west."

"It's good to make your acquaintance too. James, I hope you won't mind hearing some of these things again."

"I still find your story fascinating. Please continue."

Zeke nodded his head. "I was born in St. Louis and was basically a river rat. I didn't get much schooling. I spent most of my time catching fish and trapping critters like raccoons and beavers. After I sold the skins, I gave the money to my mother. When my pa drank too much, he beat me and my brother, and sometimes my mother. My mother passed away when I was sixteen. After that, my brother and I left home and went our separate ways.

"I convinced a fur trapper, who was heading out west, to take me with him. We left St. Louis in July 1832. I think he regarded me as a kid brother. I had no money, so Jess, the trapper, bought a horse for me. Our horses pulled his small, covered wagon all the way to what is now western Wyoming. At that time, it was just all considered the Great Plains. Two months before that, a military wagon train had set out from Missouri to cross the Great Plains and reach the Rocky Mountains. There were a hundred soldiers in the expedition. The wagons were loaded heavy with goods, so they left a well-marked trail. We followed that trail west along the Missouri River and then along the Platte River. When we came to the North Platte, we broke off the trail and headed west to the Sweetwater River."

"You were crossing Indian territory. Did any of the tribes give you trouble?" Martin asked.

"No. Sometimes we saw scouts on top of the hills, but they left us alone. We stayed well south of the Black Hills, which I expect you know is sacred to the Indians. The Lakota call it *Pahá Sápa*, which means 'hills that are black.' Over time, the Lakota became the dominant tribe there. Millions of buffalo spent the summer in those hills and the surrounding area, and the Lakota did the same.

"At that same time, south of the Black Hills, large herds of wild horses roamed the plains. After the tribes broke those mustangs, they hunted buffalo on horseback. The Lakota and their Cheyenne allies dominated the buffalo skin trade at that time. In 1831, the American Fur Company bought fifty thousand buffalo robes from the Lakota. There was a big market for them in the eastern states.

"After the Blackfeet bands learned to break mustangs, they also went after buffalo and did well. They controlled a large area of what now covers the territories of Idaho, Montana, and Wyoming. But that all changed in 1837. That year, the American Fur Company intentionally sent a small boat into Blackfeet country with traders who were infected with smallpox. They caused the death of over ten thousand Blackfeet from smallpox, and that brought about the end of their control over the buffalo trade.

"Anyway, when Jess and I reached the Sweetwater River, we built a small cabin not far from the river. We started trapping beaver that fall, when their furs became prime. Each summer an event called the American Rendezvous took place on the Green River. Pack trains hauled in trading supplies from the Missouri River, and trappers like us traded our furs for supplies to get us through the next year. Some Indians traded furs too. The rendezvous went on for several weeks. It was more than just trading. There were races, target-shooting, singing, yarn-telling, and, for some, alcohol. It was an important event for us."

"What made you decide to move to Cheyenne?" Martin wondered why a confirmed mountain man would abandon his way of life. Martin already knew he wanted to be a cowboy only as long as need be, but that was because he wanted to practice law.

"Well, the rendezvous stopped around 1840 because fur trading dropped off. Jess and I could still make a living, but it wasn't easy. Then, last year, Jess passed away, so I decided to come to Cheyenne. A friend who owns the stable here offered me a job. It's an easier life for me. I'm an old man now."

After they finished dinner, Zeke excused himself. "I expect you young fellas want to stay and talk a while longer. I rise early and need to head back to the stable. Thank you for my supper. It was a pleasure."

Martin stood up to shake Zeke's hand. "It was a pleasure to meet you. I hope to see you again."

"Would you like another sarsaparilla, James? I'm going to order a coffee."

James nodded. "Is there any talk about the Fort Laramie Treaty on the ranch?"

"Yes, I heard Doc talking about it. The final draft will be signed in early November near Fort Laramie. He said the most significant terms are that the United States Government will agree to recognize the Black Hills as part of the Great Sioux Reservation and also agree to the exclusive use of the Black Hills by the Lakota, Dakota, and Arapaho.

"In return, those tribes must agree to settle within the Black Hills reservation in the Dakota Territory. This includes the lands they fought for—the Dakota territory west of the Missouri River, the Black Hills, and the land between the Platte and the Bighorn Mountains. No whites are to be allowed into those territories. It's supposed to protect the Black Hills from white settlement. Also, the Bozeman Trail will be permanently closed.

"Doc also said that, while it all might sound fine, it's a big trade-off for the tribes. It will substantially reduce the size of their tribal lands and will make them move farther east. They'll no longer have access to their prime buffalo herds."

Jake nodded his head. "I agree with him. And for all those reasons, I think the treaty won't last long. It hasn't even been signed, and both sides aren't satisfied with the terms."

Martin slept restlessly that night, wanting to make sure he arrived at the stable before Jake did. He checked his pocket watch at midnight and rolled over. About an hour later, he woke up again, sensing his mother's presence. He felt badly about leaving the family with no explanation for his disappearance, but he didn't want his hateful brother to trace him. He needed to bide his time and build a new life.

Early the next morning, Martin helped Jake harness the horses. "It was chilly at sunrise. When does the first snowfall usually occur?"

"Sometime between late October and early November. The winters are generally mild enough for the cattle to stay out on the range. They develop very thick coats so they can still forage for grass. The watering holes don't freeze over. We might lose a few head of cattle if there's a bad blizzard, but mostly the herd survives just fine. We check on them from time to time and try to keep them from straying too far."

After they were underway, there was no more small talk. Jake focused on driving the horses, and they both watched for groundhog burrows, deep ruts, and rocks that could break a wagon wheel.

Jake knew Martin always saw James when he came to town, but he never volunteered what he did and Martin never asked him. Martin wondered if he had a lady friend. He hoped Jake did because he was a good man. When the other ranch hands came back from town, they mostly talked about going to saloons, playing cards, drinking alcohol, and dancing with the bar girls. Sometimes they raced their quarter horses. Spending time with James was all Martin was interested in doing for now.

In mid-December, Martin was reinforcing some of the corrals when Jake walked over to him. "Doc asked me to get a few things from town. The weather looks clear right now. I plan to leave early tomorrow morning and return by midafternoon. Want to keep me company?"

"Yes. Thanks for the offer. Let me know if I can help with anything."

"There are a few things you could do for me. Meet me at the stable after breakfast."

Martin hadn't been in town since October. Now partially snow-covered, the High Plains looked different. Cattle foraging on clumps of prairie grass dotted the landscape, their thick, shaggy coats insulating them from the frigid temperatures. After he and Jake agreed on a time to meet, Martin went to McGrady's General Store. When he walked in, James waved him over to the main counter. "How long will you be in town?"

"Only a few hours. I just picked up some things for Jake and was hoping you might have time for a cup of coffee."

"Yes, I could take a short break. Wait here a moment. I have something for you to take back to the ranch." James disappeared into the back room and came back carrying something cumbersome. "I ordered this for you, but it needs to stay covered until you get back to the ranch. It wouldn't be good to have this flinging around the buckboard."

"It's heavy. What did you get me?"

"It's the first book of Henry John Stephen's four books on the laws of England. I think this is the one you were saving for."

"Yes, it is. I can't thank you enough." Martin looked away and swallowed hard, fighting back tears. "No one has ever done anything like this for me. This is the doorway to my future. It'll help me pass the winter evenings. I'll repay you as soon as I can save enough."

"The only payment I'll accept is some legal advice from time to time. I'm glad to contribute to your legal career. Also, I saved you a copy of *The Cheyenne Leader* from a couple of weeks ago. It explains the terms of the Fort Laramie Treaty. There's an interesting editorial about their predictions for the treaty's success. They question how long it'll hold up and have the same concerns we discussed on your last visit."

When Martin met Jake at the buckboard, Jake pointed to the package. "What did you buy yourself?"

"This is a gift from James. It's the law book I've wanted. Now I'll be able to study on these cold winter nights."

"So you want to be a lawyer?"

"Yes, that's my goal. I expect it'll take quite a while." Martin didn't really want to discuss it. He needed to keep his job. Only James knew how deeply he desired to practice law.

Most of the ranch hands played cards to pass the long winter evenings. Doc was fine with card playing but didn't want any gambling or drinking going on in the bunkhouse. Sometimes one of the cowboys played his guitar and sang cowboy songs. As for Martin, he mostly spent the evenings devouring his law book.

In 1869, Martin bought a Cheyenne saddle, something he'd wanted for months. With its shallow seat and saddle horn that tilted forward, he could now easily slide out of the saddle to tie up a calf. He wished he'd invented it.

Most of the cowboys wore spurs, but Martin had no need for them. Blaze seemed to read his mind, anticipating everything Martin wanted him to do. Where Martin grew up, no one wore *chaparejos*, the leather seatless pants that strapped around the thighs. He liked the protection they gave him on the range. This past winter he had worn heavy, woolen angora chaps whenever he went out riding, something else he'd never seen. Living in Wyoming agreed with him. He felt a freedom here that he'd never experienced before. It was a different culture, and it agreed with him. But he did wonder if the wind would ever stop blowing. It never seemed to stop.

Martin was out on the range in July when he realized it was exactly a year ago Jake had hired him. Now twenty-one years old, he felt he'd crossed some kind of threshold. He wondered if this was how a bear feels when it comes out of hibernation, then decided a butterfly's transition from caterpillar to the freedom of wings was a more appropriate image.

He'd learned so much in the past year and gained some badly needed self-confidence. Now adept at identifying animal tracks, he checked constantly for wolf and bear tracks to safeguard the cattle, especially the calves.

One morning, he was studying a track when he noticed a tiny sparkle. Brushing aside the soil, he picked up a beautiful piece of quartz. When he had time, he wanted to experiment with using it as a pendulum. He regarded it as an auspicious sign and put it in his shirt pocket for good luck.

Before falling asleep, he always studied the stars. On clear nights, the array of stars in the Wyoming sky was spectacular. He wished his mother could see it. They shared a fascination with the night sky. She always wanted to know everything his high school teacher taught him about the planets and constellations. At a young age, Martin knew he and his mother were cut from the same cloth. He remembered walking with her in her garden at night, away from the big trees surrounding their house, the two of them marveling at the heavens above. He missed her.

Late one September afternoon, Martin was training a horse in the corral when he noticed Doc Matheson waving to him from the fence. He rode across the corral, slipped off the saddle, and nodded to Doc.

"After supper tonight come see me at the ranch house. There are a few things I'd like to talk about."

"Yes, sir."

"And bring that law book with you."

Martin nodded. "Yes, sir."

He climbed back into the saddle, wondering why Doc wanted to see his law text. After an early supper, Martin scrubbed his hands and face, picked up Stephen's *Commentaries*, and headed to the ranch house. Doc opened the front door before Martin had a chance to knock. "Good evening, Doc."

"Good evening to you. Come on in. Since I have a few questions about that book, it's best if we sit at the kitchen table. How about some coffee while we chat?"

Martin nodded. "Thank you."

"You've been here well over a year now. I keep hearing good things about you. Jake tells me you're hardworking, have good cattle sense, and get on well with the other cowboys. He also mentioned your success with training Blaze. I'm glad you could save him. Now, this is not the reason I asked you to come here and it's none of my business, but I've wondered what caused that scar near your eye. Were you in a fight?"

The question caught Martin off guard for a moment. "Not exactly. I was attacked and robbed. It was two to one. I couldn't stop them. As far as fighting goes, I stay away from bars. I think that's where most fights start."

"Well, you're right about that. So you abstain from alcohol?"

"Yes, sir. My parents were firm about that."

"What made you decide to come to Wyoming?"

"I grew up on a farm in Iowa, near the Missouri border. There were four of us brothers, too many to inherit one farm. My eldest brother was the most capable son to take over the farm. Besides, I didn't want to work the land. I've wanted to read the law since I was ten years old."

Doc nodded his head. "Now, just what are you learning in this book?"

"This is the first of four books by Henry John Stephen, an Englishman. He published his law texts in the 1840s and based them on William Blackstone's *Commentaries on the Laws of England*, which were published in 1765. Stephen organized all the statutes into a coherent system of legal principles. He also explained English common law precedents, which have been used in America since the founding of the colonies. Except, of course, we ignore any reference to the rights of royalty."

Doc laughed, and Martin relaxed somewhat. "This first book covers the rights of individuals and corporations and explains the results of cases decided by the courts. Case decisions set a legal precedent. This is important because lawyers cite case law when they're defending an individual or a business.

"This is the only volume I have. The second one addresses the rights of things, which concerns property. The third one concerns private wrongs, such as damaging a person's reputation or property. The last one involves criminal law. That's about all I can tell you. I have a lot to learn."

"Well, I wish you the best of luck with your endeavor. Jake thinks highly of you. We're in no rush to have you leave the ranch."

They talked a while longer, then Martin excused himself. He walked back to the bunkhouse, relieved to know he could stay on the ranch as long as he needed to. Doc managed his ranch operation intelligently—not only the cattle operation but also his cowhands. Martin admired him and recognized that everything he was learning would benefit him when he practiced law.

Now well into his second year on the ranch, Martin felt comfortable with the rhythm of the ranch cycle. In late summer they'd rounded up cattle from the summer pastures, bringing them closer to the ranch before the weather turned cold. Calves were weaned so the herd would be in good shape for next year's calving season. Older cows and cows who didn't produce good calves had already been sent to market.

After winter arrived, the cowboys worked to keep wolves away from the cattle and hunted deer. In mid-December, Martin was fixing supper when Jake walked into the kitchen. "I'm going to town tomorrow to pick up some supplies. If the weather holds, I plan to stay overnight. Want to come along?"

"Yes. Thanks for asking." Martin hadn't seen James for a couple of months.

The next morning, they woke to a frigid wind blowing out of the northwest. Martin and Jake drove the wagon to town, protected by a buffalo hide thrown around them. After they agreed where to meet on Sunday, Martin went straight to the bank and deposited some money into his account.

When he walked into McGrady's General Store, James waved him over. "Can you stay overnight?"

"Yes, we have a lot to talk about."

"Saturday's a busy day for us. Come back at five o'clock. We can take our time having supper. I assume you won't mind sleeping on the floor again."

"That suits me just fine."

Several hours later, they walked down the street to Ford Restaurant and sat at a back table. "Martin, I brought several copies of *The Wyoming Tribune* for you to take back to the ranch. They started publishing in November. Have you heard about the bill the governor signed on December tenth?"

"About all I know is it gave women the right to vote in Wyoming," Martin said.

"Yes. And earlier this year the Dakota Territory came within one vote of doing the same. The bill also gave voting rights to Black and Chinese males. Besides that, about a month ago the legislature passed a law guaranteeing that teachers—and most of them are women—would be paid the same as men. And they also passed a bill guaranteeing married women property rights separate from their husbands. No other state has passed this kind of legislation. This territory is enlightened compared to any other state or territory in the country."

"Thanks for the newspapers. I look forward to reading all the details. Also, I've observed something about you. Each time I see you, you look more confident."

"Now that's an accurate observation. Since Cheyenne became the territorial capital last May, new businesses keep opening. Our population is almost twenty-five hundred. McGrady's is always busy. I have no plans to leave this town. What about you?"

"I agree with you about staying here. Doc Matheson is a decent man, and Jake has taken me under his wing. They know my goal is to work for a law firm here, but they're not in any rush for me to leave the ranch. By the way, I'm halfway through the law book you gave me and have ordered the second volume."

"We took a risk when we fled here, and it was the right thing to do. You'll be practicing law before you know it. The cattle business is driving this town. You'll gain a good understanding of that business working for Doc Matheson. It'll help you be an effective lawyer."

"I agree. Also, whether it happened by accident or through fate, I will be forever thankful for meeting you on that train. I've never had a more trusted friend. By the way, there's something I've been meaning to tell you. It doesn't change anything, but my family name was actually Van Dyke. When I was sleeping in that boxcar, my maternal grandmother appeared to me in a dream. She said her name was Magdalena Handschuh. I woke instantly, knowing I had to change my family name so I couldn't be traced. That's how I came by the name Handshoe. I changed the spelling from Dutch to English. I have a half-crazed brother who'd kill me if he found me. I know it doesn't matter to you, but I just wanted you to know. I have nothing else to hide."

"I trust you also. We aren't blood brothers, but we're closer than a lot of kin. I understand why you changed your family name. You had no idea where you were going to land when you climbed into that boxcar."

"Yesterday Doc and I had an interesting talk about the Union Pacific Railroad. This year they completed a section across southern Wyoming and northern Utah. There's also a spur line running to the goldfields in western Montana. He said that along with the railroad, an army of buffalo hunters arrived. With their accurate Sharps rifles, they've managed to do what no battle commander has ever been able to accomplish. By eliminating the buffalo, they've driven the starving Lakota onto the white man's reservations. I think it's dishonorable for the U.S. government to break its treaties."

"I agree with you but I think it's only going to get worse."

4

WITH THE 1870 SPRING ROUNDUP JUST AROUND THE corner, Jake said Doc wanted the cowboys to determine where the herd had spread over the winter. The weather was clear when they all rode off in various directions. Around noon, the temperature dropped quickly and a heavy snow started falling. The stiff wind made it impossible to see clearly, but Martin caught a glimpse of some cattle heading the opposite direction of the ranch. He was sure they were seeking shelter in a gulch. Then he noticed the calf. Calves born this early often didn't survive.

Martin didn't want to abandon the cattle, especially the calf. They were part of the breeding herd Doc Matheson was developing. He rode into the ravine and managed to get them turned around. It was hard to keep them moving, but he finally got them headed back toward the ranch. He constantly circled them to keep them moving and kept the calf in the middle, close to its mother.

They were all likely to freeze to death, including him and Blaze, if they stopped moving. The wind was driving snow sideways, making it impossible to locate any landmarks. He was no longer sure he was headed in the right direction. He prayed for some kind of sign. Blaze and the cattle were plastered with icy snow, as was he. He gave complete slack to the reins and let Blaze take over.

After the sun set, Martin lost all track of time. At some

point, Blaze raised his head and whinnied, jolting Martin. Blaze picked up his pace and lowered his head against the wind. Martin discerned a soft blue light shimmering in the distance. It kept coming in and out of view. Blaze seemed to be following it.

Frigid, Martin could barely stay seated in the saddle. The blue light flickered ahead of them from time to time. At some point, the wind shifted, and he caught a glimpse of the corral. They weren't far from the main barn. He dismounted and, after managing to open the corral gate, slipped to the ground. The cattle passed through the gate and headed for shelter near the barn. Grabbing Blaze's reins, Martin pulled himself up and stumbled forward.

One of the ranch hands came running out of the bunkhouse and grabbed Martin. "I'll take care of Blaze and the cattle. Get into the bunkhouse right now. The temperature must be near thirty below. What were you doing out there?"

"I thought I could round up these strays before the storm hit. If not for Blaze, I would have died out there."

Martin stumbled into the bunkhouse and changed into dry clothes. One of the cowboys grabbed Martin's buffalo hide, threw it in front of the fireplace, and told Martin to lie down and wrap it around him.

"We need to get your circulation going. You're damned lucky to be alive." One of the old hands started rubbing Martin's extremities. "Tell the cook to heat up some leftovers. Those angora chaps saved you."

Martin's scarf had protected most of his face. His fingers and toes hurt the most, the pain running deep into his bones. When the cook approached him with a small bottle of whiskey, Martin refused to take any.

"You have to take some. You're starting to cough. There's congestion in your chest. I'll mix it with some hot water. You must take this."

Martin accepted the cook's whiskey concoction and had

to admit he felt it working its way into his chest. He couldn't remember the last time he'd felt this exhausted—maybe when he fled Chicago after the attack, but that was a different kind of exhaustion. He knew he'd come close to dying tonight. For the second time, death had approached him and turned away.

The next morning, Jake said Doc Matheson wanted to see him after the storm stopped. The wind was still blowing sideways, piling snow drifts against all the buildings. That afternoon, after checking on Blaze, Martin walked to the ranch house. The fences and buildings were plastered with snow. He'd never seen anything quite like it. He still felt exhausted, too exhausted to feel nervous about going to Doc's house.

The maid opened the front door and led Martin to the family room. When he and Doc talked about legal things, it was usually out on the front porch or, if it was cold, in his office. This was the first time Doc had invited him into the family's living space. A fire roared in the stone fireplace that ran from floor to ceiling.

"I've never seen such a beautiful fireplace."

"It's made of river rocks and boulders. There's nothing better than nature when it comes to creating beauty. Now, Martin, tell me about the conditions when the blizzard started to blow in."

"Doc, in the time I've spent on your ranch, I've never seen a storm blow in this fast. When the temperature started falling, five head of cattle broke away and headed into a ravine for shelter. When I saw the calf, I was sure it wouldn't survive the storm, so I went after them. I tied them loosely together and wrapped the lead around my saddle horn to get them to move. By that time, the snow was falling fast, and the wind was howling.

"Blaze understood better than I just how serious the situation was. He kept neighing, louder than I've ever heard him. He pulled hard on the lead, forcing the cattle to follow. I had no idea he was so strong. Without Blaze guiding us, we wouldn't have made it back.

"I don't know how we could have predicted such a severe storm was headed our way. A frontiersman told me that Indian tribes have lore about these kinds of things. They study nature closely and notice anything that varies from its normal routine. They observe the condition of the prairie grasses. They keep track of bird migrations and bear hibernations; if they occur early, they know the winter will probably be harsh."

"Well, those are good thoughts. After this storm passes, I'd like you and Jake to talk to the cowhands and see if they noticed anything unusual last fall. You have a way with words. Just write down their observations and bring them to me."

When he walked back to the bunkhouse, Martin realized he'd wanted to give the calf a chance to survive, just like the old man in Chicago had given him. He felt he was giving back, but to what or to whom, he wasn't sure.

In early April, Martin went into town with Jake to get supplies and spend the night. After depositing his salary in his bank account, he walked into McGrady's General Store.

James waved him over to the counter. "I've been wondering when I'd see you again. I can leave soon. Let's have supper at Ford Restaurant."

After they were seated, James said, "It's been almost four years since we arrived in Cheyenne. That scar near your eye has healed well. It's no longer the first thing one notices about you."

"Well, I'll take that as a compliment, but I still feel branded by it. It reminds me of the day I lost my family's farm. When I left for Chicago, my father was so weak that I expect he has passed on. It's my mother and youngest brother I'm most concerned about. I went to Western Union today and wired money to her without giving my name. I intend to repay every cent that was stolen from me, and then some."

"Martin, the only way we could create a new life was to leave our families behind. We're both on quite a journey. I've made a number of acquaintances through the store, but you're the only person I trust completely."

"Likewise. I know I can depend on you."

"By the way, have you heard that Governor Campbell appointed a woman as Justice of the Peace in South Pass City? Esther Morris is the first female to hold public office in the entire country. She has a one-year appointment."

"No. I wasn't aware of that. News takes time to reach the ranch. That should attract some women to Wyoming."

James smiled. "Yes, it should. We certainly could do with that."

"I spent an hour with Michael McCann this afternoon. Thank you again for the introduction. The growing cattle business is keeping him and his law partner very busy. He said I should stop by whenever I get to town. He also said if his practice keeps growing, he might be able to hire me in a couple of years. In the meantime, he's willing to discuss case law with me whenever I have any questions. It's only because of your friendship with him that he's willing to do this. I can't thank you enough."

"Martin, all I did was make the introduction. Your dedication to reading the law is quite apparent. Also, there's a certain reserve about you that I believe would appeal to a law firm and its clients."

On the way back to James's place that night, Martin noticed Will, one of the young cowboys from the ranch, being roughed up outside a bar. "James, I need to stop that." Martin crossed the street and pulled an older cowboy off his friend. "What do you think you're doing?"

"He walked out and didn't leave enough to pay for his drinks. I'm just teaching him a lesson to never do that again."

"Tell me how much he owes you, and I'll give it to you."

After the cowboy walked away, Martin turned to Will. "I hope you will not have to learn that lesson again."

"I was sure I had enough money. Thank you for stopping him. He would have beat me to a pulp."

Martin nodded his head. "See you at the ranch tomorrow." He walked back across the street to James. "That's why I have nothing to do with alcohol.

Martin was breaking in a yearling when he noticed the housekeeper heading to the corral, waving to catch his attention. He rode over to her, dismounted, and tied up the horse.

"What can I do for you?"

"Doc wants to see you at the ranch house when you finish working with the horse."

"Tell him I'll be there within an hour. Do you have any idea what it concerns?"

"No, I don't."

Martin decided there was nothing to worry about. After he released the horse into a paddock, he changed his shirt and headed to the ranch house. The housekeeper was waiting at the front door and showed him to Doc's study.

"Take a seat, Martin. How are you managing with that yearling?"

"He's strong and a bit stubborn, but he'll be good on the range. I just need to work with him a bit longer."

"Are you planning to see your friend McCann any time soon?"

"I'm going into town Saturday morning to see James. I could stop by McCann's office for you."

"I've written down a few things I'd like you to ask him."

"I'm glad to do that. He thinks highly of you."

"I know that before long you'll leave the ranch to practice law, and I think you'll do well. You're not the type to pull a fast one on anyone. Too many lawyers look for ways to abuse the law and are willing to do almost anything to make an almighty dollar. I predict you'll have a reputation for your honesty and intelligence."

"Thanks, Doc. I appreciate you saying that."

Walking back to the bunkhouse, Martin thought about Cheyenne's growth over the past seven years. Besides being the territorial capital, it was a significant center for banking and the cattle industry. There were seventy bars spread across town, not that Martin ever went into any of them. When he went to town, he usually spent time at McCann's office discussing legal issues and how to approach them. McCann was grooming Martin to be part of his law firm. The firm's number of clients was growing steadily.

Besides wanting to practice law, Martin had another reason for living in Cheyenne. He wanted to have a family of his own one day. As a cowboy, it was nearly impossible to meet a woman, much less marry her. Working as a lawyer could change all that. Sometimes he daydreamed about how it would feel to have a woman who loved him, what it would be like to have children.

None of that was within reach now but, when it did happen, he vowed to never treat his children the way his father had treated him and his brothers. He'd been strict to the point of harshness. Martin could only remember a few times that his father had praised him for something. In his small Dutch town, parents didn't want to foster pride in their children. They considered it sinful.

Thank heaven his mother was an exception. Her kindness to him was etched in his memory. She understood he was different from his older brothers and quietly encouraged him to pursue his interests. She said to never judge someone unless you'd walked in their shoes. He wanted to find a woman of similar spirit. Someone who was kind to others, someone who would stand by him, someone who would love him in spite of his faults.

A few days later, Jake waved Martin over to one of the corrals. "I want to share a few words with you in private. Doc just told me his wife's nephew Jed will start working with us tomorrow. He doesn't sound happy about it. He said Jed has trouble keeping a job and to keep an eye on him. He also said to treat him like any other cowhand and let Doc know if he causes any trouble."

"Thanks for the warning. I'll keep my distance."

"Let me know if you see or hear anything that could be a problem."

"I'll be sure to do that."

Martin observed how Jed treated the other cowboys and how hard he actually worked. Initially things went all right but, after a few months, his behavior changed. Jed looked irritated, almost angry, that he was expected to earn his keep.

The middle of May was roundup time with the cowboys working sixteen to eighteen hours a day. After rounding up stray cattle on the open range, the calves were branded, counted, and then released back on the range. Over the summer, Martin managed to avoid any close contact with Jed.

In late August of 1876, Martin hoped to be employed at McCann's law firm by the following summer. He was thinking about it over breakfast when Jake came into the cookhouse. "I'm going to Cheyenne tomorrow and plan to spend the night. Want to come along?"

"Yes. Thanks. I haven't seen James for a while. I'll be waiting for you at the stable."

After the ride into town, they agreed where to meet the next morning and went their separate ways. Two years prior, James had purchased a small cabin not far from the business district. In return for staying there, Martin always treated James to dinner at Ford Restaurant. He'd never trusted anyone as much as he trusted James. Like a stream carving out a riverbed, the bond of their friendship ran deeper each year.

When Martin entered McGrady's General Store, James waved him over. "Are you staying in town tonight?"

"Yes. I wanted to stop here before I go to McCann's office. There's some research he wants me to do. I'll meet you at Ford Restaurant at five o'clock. I want to hear everything you know about the Battle of the Little Bighorn."

Martin arrived early, requested their usual table, and ordered a sarsaparilla for James and hot tea for himself. When James came in, he set down the newspapers he'd tucked under his arm. "These are for you to take back to the ranch. More details keep being revealed about what happened at Little Bighorn."

"Thanks for saving them. It'll be helpful to read about what happened instead of just hearing rumors. What documents do you have in your satchel?"

"They aren't really documents. I've been cutting out articles from *The Wyoming Tribune* that would jog my memory of things I want to talk to you about." James pulled out a handful of newspaper clippings and set them on the table. "These all relate to the various treaties that have been made and broken. In 1849 when the army established Fort Laramie, there'd already been a steady stream of Euro-American migrants crossing Sioux territory to get to the Oregon Territory. The tribes weren't happy about it, but at least the migrants kept moving west.

"Then in 1868, the year we arrived here, the Lakota and Northern Cheyenne signed the Treaty of Fort Laramie with the U.S. government. The treaty guaranteed that their tribal reservation would include the Black Hills and a large area in the Montana and Wyoming Territories. Also, by that time, some leaders like Red Cloud and Spotted Tail had already set-tled their communities on reservations outside the Black Hills and were dependent on the government for food and various goods."

"Yes," Martin said. "I remember that Crazy Horse immedi-ately disapproved of the Fort Laramie Treaty. I think it mostly held together until Custer's soldiers found gold in the Black Hills in 1874. Then all bets were off as hordes of prospectors descended on Sioux land."

"That's right. Custer's expedition was supposed to deter-mine where the army should build a fort near the Black Hills, but an unstated purpose of the trip was to determine if the rumors of gold deposits were true. They camped in the Black Hills for about a week and found gold on top of the ground and in the streams. Custer was well aware the deposits were in Lakota territory, but it's interesting that he neglected to men-tion it in his report. It was the reporters traveling with the expeditions who spread the word across the country."

Martin shook his head. "I forgot that. I do remember the government tried to purchase the Black Hills from the Cheyenne, Arapaho, and Lakota. The proposed treaty called for reducing the amount of tribal land and excluding the Black Hills from their reservations. A majority of the tribal members refused the offer, claiming they'd been guaranteed ownership of the Black Hills under previous treaties. I think that still stands."

"Early in 1875, the U.S. government ordered the Cheyenne, Arapaho, and Lakota to cede their territory and negotiate the sale of their reservations by January thirty-first, 1876. That fall the Cheyenne, Blackfeet, Hunkpapa, and eight Lakota bands met to discuss selling the Black Hills. Little Big Man threatened to shoot anyone who wanted to sell the Black Hills. Young Man Afraid, an Indian policeman, brought the situation under control, but the meeting ended with no res-olution. The bargainers never agreed on a specific amount to demand from the government for the Black Hills."

Martin sighed. "So the tribes still haven't signed an agreement with the United States government about selling their reservations."

"That's right," James said and picked up one of the newspapers. "This March, many Lakota, Northern Cheyenne, and Arapaho traveled north to meet with Sitting Bull and the Hunkpapa at Little Bighorn. They were planning a sun dance ceremony and a big hunt in eastern Montana. By early June, their camp near the Rosebud River numbered in the thousands. In mid-June, General Crook and his force were approaching the area when Sitting Bull and Crazy Horse led an attack against them. Many were killed on both sides. At the end of the day, the tribes returned to their camp, and Crook accepted the fact that the Indian force was too large for his troops to defeat.

"Then, on June twenty-fifth and twenty-sixth, General Custer and the 7th Cavalry attacked the tribes. The battle took place along the Little Bighorn River. This article says Custer's Crow scouts warned him the Indian encampment was the largest they'd ever seen. They told him they could all die if they attacked the tribes in the valley below. Custer, who was reputed to be the army's most aggressive general, refused to delay the attack. On hearing this, Mitch Bouyer, one of Custer's most trusted scouts, told a much younger scout to leave and seek safety.

"The Lakota leader, Gall, whose wife and daughter were killed early in the battle, led a thousand warriors in pursuit of Custer. The battle was a complete rout for Custer and his troops. Not one of the 7th Cavalry survived.

"In response to this, the United States Congress attached a rider to the August fifteenth Indian Appropriations Bill. It nullified the Fort Laramie Treaty of 1868, which had pledged the Black Hills to the Sioux Nation. All rations and payments to the Lakota will cease until they stop hostilities and cede the Black Hills to the United States."

Martin cracked his knuckles. "I can't help but wonder where White Wolf is camped and how he's faring—or if he's still alive. The tribes depended upon buffalo for their livelihood but that's now impossible because of the wholesale slaughter urged by the government. Buffalo are shot from trains for sport and left to rot. At one time there were roughly 30,000,000 buffalo. Now only a few hundred remain. Perhaps President Grant thinks it's the solution to the country's Indian problem. I read that Major General William Tecumseh Sherman said that as long as the Sioux are allowed to hunt buffalo, they'll never surrender to a plow."

James picked up another paper. "The proposed Agreement of 1877 will force tribes onto reservations early next year. The Lakota will be required to renounce their claim to the Black Hills. The Red Cloud Agency will be relocated to the southwest Dakota Territory and will be called the Pine Ridge Reservation. It is said to be dry and dusty, the soil infertile, and there are no good streams.

"The tribes are being offered 4.5 million dollars to abandon their land claims. Either they accept the treaty or face starvation. After that, it will be legal for settlers to claim the land they've resided on for the past couple of years."

"James, do you think the U.S. government's unstated policy is the extermination of all the tribes?"

"Well, perhaps not outright annihilation, but they are hellbent on dehumanizing them. I don't agree with it."

With the arrival of spring, the cowboys were staying out on the range for longer periods of time. On the few evenings Martin came back to the ranch, Doc sometimes asked him to come and sit on his front porch. They usually discussed legal issues, but it was clear to Martin that Doc simply enjoyed his company. Several times Martin caught Jed, the nephew of Doc's wife, glaring at him and stomping away when Martin returned to the bunkhouse. There was no mistaking his jealousy of Martin's relationship with Doc. The other cowboys knew Martin would leave the ranch one day and understood Doc just liked to talk to him about the law. Martin worked as hard as the rest of them, maybe even harder. They had no problem with him.

Early one morning, Jake stopped Martin just as he was heading out to the range. "Martin, there's something I want to warn you about. Are you aware that Jed's jealous of you?"

"Not exactly, but I know he's never liked me. I try to steer clear of him."

"Make sure you keep doing that. Several of the ranch hands said he's jealous because Doc likes spending time with you. He would burn your law books if he could get away with it."

"Does Doc have any idea about this?"

"He's usually a good judge of character, but I don't believe he knows how bad the situation is. There's something wrong with Jed. Doc felt obligated to hire him, but I can tell he doesn't trust him. Not one of the wranglers likes him. We all tread carefully because Jed's related to Doc's wife Etta. I'm warning you to watch your back. Jed's an angry man. There's a dark side to him."

"Jake, I want to tell you something that happened earlier this week. I was rounding up a stray calf when the strangest thing happened. I was heading into a gulch to rope the calf when the hair on the back of my neck prickled. I sensed some kind of threat. I turned around in the saddle and saw Jed aiming his rifle at me. At that moment, my bunkmate, who was making a ride back to check on me, came riding up behind Jed. When Jed saw him, he immediately lowered his rifle and said he thought he saw a rattlesnake. There was no rattlesnake."

"Make sure you're never alone on the range. When I find the right moment, I'll talk to Doc about this."

That night, Martin camped close to the chuck wagon. Before falling asleep, he pulled Oma's pendant out of his saddlebag. He only consulted it when he wanted to confirm his intuition about something. But tonight was different. He felt he was in danger and was searching for an answer. After determining which way it was swinging, he mentally asked if Jed wanted to kill him. The pendulum swung firmly in the direction it had chosen for yes.

With that confirmation, he decided to leave the ranch immediately. Early in the morning, he ate at the chuck wagon and then rode off as if it were a normal day on the range. After making sure no one could see him, he headed in the direction of Cheyenne.

When he entered McGrady's General Store through the back door, James spotted him and nodded for Martin to wait a moment.

"You never come into town this early. Has something happened?"

"The situation with Jed has become serious, deadly serious. There was another incident with him this week. I can't return to the ranch. Jake thinks he wants to kill me. I need to find a different job. The last time I talked to Michael McCann, he said it was still too soon to hire me, that it might take another six to twelve months. I can't wait that long. Besides, I'm not sure I'd even feel safe in Cheyenne. I don't think Jed's jealousy would end if I left the ranch. I haven't told Doc anything. I don't want to put him in an impossible situation."

"Your timing's interesting. A customer came in late yesterday, looking for one or two more cowboys to help him drive some cattle to the Dakota Territory. A town called Spearfish has been established on the periphery of the Black Hills. His property will lie north of the town. He's coming back around one o'clock to see if I could find anyone to help him. If you decide to do this, I want to have a long talk with you tonight. You may sleep in the back room here, and Blaze can stay in the sheltered area behind the store."

"Thank you. I need to go to the bank and take care of a few things. I won't be gone long."

On the way to the bank, Martin pressed his left hand against his right wrist, slowing his pulse. He needed to think clearly. He didn't like what he'd heard about the mining of gold in the Black Hills. When it came to the desire for land and gold, the U.S. government had no difficulty violating its treaties. The Black Hills wasn't somewhere he would choose to live, but, confound it, he had no better alternative.

James was helping a customer when Martin returned that afternoon. He nodded to Martin, then motioned with his head toward a man standing near the front counter. Martin remembered seeing him before. His presence was different from the average man walking down the streets of Cheyenne. He carried himself very erectly, his boots polished and his western attire freshly laundered. Martin wondered what he'd look like on a cattle drive.

Martin walked over to him. "Good afternoon. My name is Martin Handshoe. I believe you're Andrew Sanborn."

"Yes. Pleased to meet you. James said you'd be willing to drive cattle to the Dakota Territory. He assured me you have considerable experience with handling them and that your horse is well-trained. I could use your talents. Will you help me?"

"Yes, I will."

"Lawrence County was created in 1875 by the Dakota Territory Legislature. About a year ago, the Spearfish Townsite Company selected a site along Spearfish Creek to develop a small town. A number of lots have already been bought for businesses. Before long it'll be a bustling cattle town. The name 'Spearfish' comes from the Lakota tribe. They've speared fish in the river for a very long time. My ranch will lie north of Spearfish. The drive will start early tomorrow. Meet me at the stockyards at six o'clock."

Sanborn extended his hand, and Martin shook it. "I'll be

there. Thank you for hiring me."

Sanborn nodded his head. "There'll be room in the camp wagon for you to store a few belongings. What kind of guns do you carry?"

"I have a Colt 45 sidearm and a Winchester 30-30 rifle."

"Good. Until tomorrow morning."

Martin went out the back door and sat down on a bench near Blaze to take stock of his situation. Given his escape to Wyoming, he understood the mental and physical energy required to create a new life, but he was young enough to do it again. If he could never return to Cheyenne, he'd find a way to practice law in Spearfish. The cattle business drove that town's economy, and that was a world he understood.

Shortly after the store closed, James bought some biscuits and ham for their supper. They ate in the back of the shop, leaving the back door open so Blaze could see them.

"I'm sure Sanborn's chuck wagon will be well-stocked, but here's some hardtack for you to carry in your saddlebag," James said. "I expect Jake will explain to Doc why you had to leave the ranch, and I'm sure it won't surprise him. Someday, when Doc brings your law books to me, I'll answer any questions he might have."

"Thank you. I hope you're right about everything. I wrote a letter to Doc this afternoon, explaining why I had to leave. He's always been fair to me, and I owe him an explanation for my decision. Please give this to him when he stops by the store. I'll miss him."

James nodded. "We'll both miss you. I'll keep your law books until you tell me to send them. Stagecoaches are already running a couple of times a week to Deadwood." He spread a map across a bench. "This map shows the Dakota and Wyoming Territories. I expect you'll drive the cattle almost due north and then shift to the northeast when you get near the Black Hills. At some point before that, you'll have to cross the North Platte River." James ran his finger along the river line. "There should be grasslands most of the way to Spearfish."

"Here's what concerns me. We both know the situation in the Black Hills has changed drastically in the past couple of years. When it comes to gold, treaties don't mean anything. I expect the ranch is on land that was part of the Great Sioux Reservation."

"You really have no choice but to go on the cattle drive."

"I understand. I'm just being honest with you. I'll miss Cheyenne, and I'll miss your company. I've never had a better friend than you."

"We're more than friends. We're brothers. I'm closer to you than I ever was to any of my siblings. This isn't goodbye. We'll see each other again. It just might take a while for that to happen."

After James left, Martin spread a blanket on the ground near Blaze and slept fitfully. He got up at five o'clock the next morning, fed Blaze, ate a couple of biscuits, and headed to the stockyards. Despite his misgivings about leaving Cheyenne, he was thankful Sanborn had hired him. This cattle drive was a chance for Martin to prove his worth and also lay the foundation for a new life.

Fate seemed to have intervened in his life once again, and this time it would be far different than his flight to Wyoming. He was older, had financial reserves in a bank, and had started reading the law. Maybe this cattle drive would prove to be the opportunity he'd been waiting for.

5

WHEN MARTIN ARRIVED AT THE STOCKYARD, SANBORN was already there. "Thanks for getting here early. There's someone I want you to meet before we leave. Miguel and two vaqueros he knows have agreed to help with the cattle drive. After we get to the ranch, they'll head back to Santa Fe. They're experienced cattlemen, and we're fortunate to have their assistance."

He waved Miguel over. "Miguel, this is Martin. For now, Miguel will take the lead and make sure the herd keeps moving in the right direction. Martin, I want you to bring up the rear and keep checking for stragglers."

Martin extended his hand. "Pleased to meet you, Miguel."

Before they left the stockyard, Sanborn called all the cowboys together. "It should take roughly forty days to reach Spearfish. We won't drive the cattle hard. I want them to gain some weight when we pass through the grasslands. If you have questions at any time, don't hesitate to ask me about your concerns. We all need to help each other."

Working roundups on Doc's ranch was one thing, but driving a hundred head of cattle for forty days exceeded anything Martin had ever undertaken. It only took a couple of days for him to understand why Sanborn had hired Miguel and his friends. They were hardworking and clearly very experienced with driving cattle for long distances. On the tenth day of the drive, the herd was approaching the North Platte

River. Martin was keeping a close watch on the western sky and didn't like the looks of the clouds massing on the horizon. He turned and noticed Sanborn riding his horse at a gallop toward him.

"Handshoe, I'm watching those clouds too. We need to get the cattle across the North Platte before that storm strikes. I've asked Miguel and his vaqueros to drop back and help round up any stragglers. I want you to join them and follow Miguel's lead. According to the map, we should be close to a narrow crossing. We need to move quickly. Everyone needs to get their ponchos on."

Martin nodded. "I'll follow Miguel's lead and support him in any way I can."

When Miguel rode to the back of the herd, the other vaqueros also dropped back to move the herd faster. Martin was impressed. Everyone worked in concert. He and Miguel stayed in the rear, going after any head of cattle that tried to stray from the herd.

The towering clouds heading toward them unnerved Martin. He knew from his years on Doc's ranch just how powerful these storms could be. Surviving them out on the range was one thing; driving cattle across a river like the North Platte was quite another. They needed to ford the river before the storm broke loose, sending lightning strikes over all of them. His heart raced at the thought of it. He forced himself to focus on getting the cattle above the waterline on the far bank.

Suddenly Blaze slowed his pace and kept trying to veer off toward a gully. Martin reined him back in the direction of the cattle, but Blaze continued to balk and shake his head. Finally Martin signaled to Miguel that he was going after some stragglers. He gave Blaze free rein, and Blaze quickly turned into the gully. He ran at a gallop, only stopping short when he saw five head of cattle grazing along the creek bed.

Martin leaned forward and patted Blaze on his neck. "I

should have trusted you right from the start. I owe you an apology. Let's round them up."

At those words, they headed into the creek bed and forced the cattle to turn around. By the time they reached the North Platte, most of the cattle were on the other side. Miguel rode back and helped Martin drive the stragglers across the river.

Just as they reached the other side, a blinding rain started to fall, unnerving the cattle. Miguel signaled for Martin to follow him in the direction he was heading. Sanborn was motioning to drive the herd toward a bluff. After several hours, the wind's force dropped off, but rain continued to fall in sheets. They spent the night at the base of the bluff, taking shifts to keep the cattle from straying.

A stunning sunrise stirred everyone to life. Martin got some coffee from the chuck wagon and carried a mug over to Miguel. "Good morning. It seems Mother Nature is trying to make amends for the storm last night."

Miguel smiled and nodded, then pointed to Sanborn, who was walking over to them.

"Give your crew my thanks for bringing up the stragglers yesterday. From here on we'll drive the cattle due north and keep moving through the Wyoming grasslands. We won't drive them hard. I'll see you at camp tonight. Thank heaven there are no storm clouds on the horizon."

Martin's respect for Sanborn increased with each passing day. He was as dust-covered and hardworking as everyone else. He asked nothing of the cowboys that he wasn't willing to do himself. Everyone respected him. Martin was learning a thing or two about leadership. Sometimes a gift comes in an unexpected package.

During the third week of the drive, Martin noticed a perceptible difference in the elevation. The air felt thinner, lighter. The grasslands were lush compared to the rangeland near Cheyenne. In the distance, to the northeast, the land looked elevated and darker.

When they camped that night, he walked over to Sanborn and pointed to the northeast. "Is that dark mass the Black Hills?"

"Yes. Good observation. They'll be more prominent in a few days. Before long we'll see some interesting buttes. An uprising of molten lava created them long ago. We'll pass closest to the one known as Devil's Tower. The Lakota call it '*Mato Tipila*,' which means 'Bear Butte Lodge.' We'll take our time moving past it. Spearfish is a day or two northeast of there. The ranch will lie north of town."

Several days later, Devil's Tower rose above the horizon. It was the most intriguing structure Martin had ever seen. He wished they could pass closer before heading to Spearfish Valley. After they started driving the herd east, Martin kept looking back at the butte, trying to imprint it in his memory. When they entered the Spearfish River Valley, its beauty captivated Martin. The landscape was a stark contrast to southern Wyoming. There'd been a storm the previous night, and the river was running fast. Martin inhaled deeply, drawing pine-scented air deep into his lungs.

At camp that night, Sanborn pulled out a notebook from his saddlebag, drew a map of their location, and showed it to the cowboys. "We're due north of the Spearfish Townsite. This is where we'll stake out the land claim tomorrow. The following day I'll go to Spearfish with Cook Wagner to register the claim and get supplies for us. I'll also arrange for some logs to be brought there. The bunkhouse and kitchen will be built first, then the stable.

"One more thing. I thank each one of you for your hard work. Our vaqueros are heading back to the Territory of New Mexico tomorrow. We'll gather around the campfire tonight and have a final supper with them. I know we all wish them safe travels. The cattle drive went better than I dared hope it would, and that's because of each one of you."

That evening, Martin looked at the cowboys sitting around

the fire. Even though covered with trail dust and exhausted from the long journey, they looked pleased with themselves. Sanborn was a good leader. The men respected him, as did Martin. He considered himself fortunate to have worked for Doc Matheson and now Sanborn. He hoped Doc wouldn't judge him harshly once he'd had a chance to talk to James and read Martin's letter.

Two days later, before Sanborn and Cook Wagner left for Spearfish, Sanborn marked the area he wanted cleared for a small cabin, bunkhouse, stable, and lean-to. "Since the vaqueros left, there are only eight of us. With these buildings, we should manage just fine. Cook and I will bring back some supper from town for you."

When he returned late that afternoon, Sanborn gathered everyone around the firepit. "First of all, not only did you clear the area for the bunkhouse and stable, but you also managed to cut some logs for us to sit on. You accomplished all that faster than I thought was possible. Thank you for your hard work. When I was in town, I arranged to have logs delivered here within the next day or two. That company will also help us construct the buildings.

"Spearfish was founded just over a year ago and now has about 150 settlers. One of the first things the founders built was a small stockade to protect the town from the harsh winters and from any raids. There's also a U.S. Post Office and a log cabin that serves as the local school. Some stores have opened, including a café and a saloon. You're welcome to ride into town on Friday and Saturday nights and stay overnight if you want. We just can't all go there at the same time."

The first time Martin went into town, he rode Blaze around the outskirts of Spearfish, exploring possible sites for a small cabin. Until he could actually purchase some land, he wanted to carry an image in his mind. When he tried to turn Blaze back toward main street, Blaze shook his head and insisted on heading farther west. Martin's relationship with Blaze ran deep. He trusted Blaze's intuition about herding cattle and finding lost steers. Also, he had to admit Blaze always found his way back home when they went off course to track down strays. Martin sighed and gave him free rein.

Within half a mile, Blaze halted under a stand of ponderosa pines. Below them, a small creek ran through a field of prairie grass. Ponderosas blanketed the hills on the other side of the creek. A gentle breeze rustled through the pines, softly brushing Martin's face and playing lightly with Blaze's mane. "Blaze, is this where you want me to build your stable one day?"

Blaze snuffled and shook his head.

Martin smiled. "Did the scent of that meadow lead you here? Be patient. When the time is right, I'll see if this might be possible."

After riding around Spearfish, Martin bought a copy of the *Black Hills Pioneer* and ordered supper at a small café. When he finished reading the paper and eating, he headed back to the ranch. There was no reason for him to spend the night in Spearfish. The bars held no attraction for him, not only because he didn't touch alcohol, but also because fights broke out between cowboys far too easily. He wanted no part of it. Spearfish was a cattle town; if not as rough as Deadwood, it was a close second. Cowboys and miners were no strangers to gunfights and fistfights.

When Martin was alone on the range, he sometimes felt that someone or something was watching him. He sensed the presence was human rather than animal and felt a bit unsettled by it, but not threatened. Thinking about someone observing him with interest rather than intending any harm made him curious.

In early August, Martin was trailing cattle along Spearfish

Creek when he again felt someone observing him. No other cowboys were working this section of the ranch, so it couldn't be one of them. Without turning around, he left some pemmican and biscuits on a rock. Then he swung himself up onto Blaze and headed upstream. After a couple of minutes, he turned around. The food was gone.

This occurred several more times, always near a gulley that snaked along Spearfish Creek. He'd once read that even a hunter cannot kill a bird that flies to him for refuge. It was a beautiful thought. He'd never experienced a creature coming to him in some kind of need. When he let his mind wander, the image of a Lakota came to him. Once Martin decided the man was tracking him because he was hungry, he no longer felt unsettled. This land had belonged to the Lakota for centuries. They knew the locations of the best fishing spots and watering holes and where they were most likely to find game. Their problem now was that the U.S. government had seized most of their tribal lands.

Martin decided to get some tobacco to carry in his saddlebag. He wanted to be able to offer some to the Lakota if he ever had the chance to meet him.

Martin thought about the clairvoyance he'd felt as a young boy. It usually came to him when there was a possibility of danger. One summer afternoon, he'd sensed that a strong storm was coming. He ran to find his parents and brothers and tell them they had to go to the storm cellar. It was broad daylight, but within minutes the sky darkened and debris started flying through the air. The family barely made it into the storm cellar before the storm hit.

Martin felt absolutely no sense of danger with the perceptions he was receiving about the Lakota. He wondered how they would meet and how long it would take for that to happen. He didn't question the source of his clairvoyance. He just knew it happened, and he trusted it.

In mid-September, Martin again sensed the Lakota's presence. He wrapped some biscuits and pemmican in a bandana and set the food on a rock. After riding away a short distance, Martin turned around and saw a native holding the parcel. Martin extended his right palm to the Indian. The Lakota did the same, then rode away on his horse.

A week later, Martin was tracking a steer not far from the spot where he'd seen the Lakota. He stopped under a scrubby pine so Blaze could rest and take a drink from the creek. He also wanted to get out of the sun and out of the saddle for a while. He'd just sat down on a large boulder when a sharp crack rang out. A bullet boomeranged off the boulder, striking close to Martin. He leaped down to the ground, his heart pumping hard. Blaze was snorting and shaking his head. Martin looked back and saw a dead rattlesnake at the base of the boulder.

When he looked around to see where the shot had come from, the Lakota was walking toward them, his rifle slung over his shoulder. Martin raised his arm and extended his palm in greeting. The Lakota stopped about ten feet from Martin and did the same.

Martin pointed to his chest. "Handshoe." He touched the top of his right hand with his left forefinger and said, "Hand," then he pointed to his boot. "Shoe."

The man pointed to his chest. "*Šunkmánitu tánka ska*. White Wolf."

"You know English?"

"Some."

"You saved my life. Thank you for killing that rattlesnake."

White Wolf pointed to the scar on Martin's face.

Martin rolled back his left sleeve and showed the jagged scar running up his lower arm. "Someone tried to kill me. You understand?"

White Wolf nodded.

"Where's your horse?"

White Wolf pointed to a tree downstream from them.

It took a moment for Martin to discern the horse behind some bushes. The horse was perfectly quiet.

White Wolf nodded, and there was just a hint of a smile.

"I'm tracking a steer." Martin pointed to the hoofprints.

White Wolf pointed across the creek and a bit upstream.

"Thank you." Martin raised his right forefinger. "Wait." He raised his right hand and faced his palm toward White Wolf.

Blaze took a few steps toward Martin. "This is Blaze. He also saved my life."

When White Wolf extended his hand, Blaze walked over to him, nuzzled his hand, and nickered.

Martin observed Blaze closely. He seemed to comprehend what had just occurred. Martin opened his saddlebag and took out some hardtack. He offered it to White Wolf, then reached into the saddlebag again. He pulled out the tobacco pouch and offered it to White Wolf. "Thank you again."

White Wolf nodded, accepting the pouch and hardtack. Martin watched him walk toward his horse. When he was about halfway there, White Wolf made some kind of signal and his horse started walking toward him. Martin had never seen anything quite like it. White Wolf grasped the single rein that extended from the bit and swung himself onto his horse's back. Horse and rider looked seamless.

Sanborn had told him the Lakota didn't use saddles and never whipped their horses. Rather than pulling on the rein to get his horse moving, White Wolf raised his knees to signal he wanted to leave. When they reached the top of the hill, he leaned back and his horse stopped immediately. He looked at Martin for a few moments, then turned around and leaned forward slightly. His horse responded immediately, moving in the direction White Wolf was looking, and they disappeared over the hill.

Martin was fascinated. White Wolf had given no voice

command. His leaning one way or the other was all the direction his horse required. Respect rather than domination seemed to be the guiding principle. Martin had always tried to be gentle with Blaze, especially after the mistreatment by his previous owner, but White Wolf's communication with his horse was far more subtle.

Not long after the incident with White Wolf, Martin was about to head out to the range when he saw Sanborn and Cook Wagner returning from an overnight stay in Spearfish. "Cook, could I help you unload those supplies?"

"I'd appreciate it."

"Martin, after you finish with that, would you round up the cowboys? Cook is planning to make a tasty supper for us. I brought back a copy of *The Black Hills Pioneer*. I think everyone will be interested in hearing the latest news."

Late that afternoon, with everyone gathered around the campfire, Sanborn stood up. "This past May, Crazy Horse brought his people into Red Cloud Agency, just outside Fort Robinson, Nebraska. They came in under a flag of truce. Nine hundred of Crazy Horse's people came with him, along with over two thousand horses. The last winter on the range was so brutal they could barely survive it."

Chef raised his hand. "It didn't help that the government basically exterminated the buffalo, their main food source, over the past few years."

"That's right, Chef. And it gets more complicated." Sanborn held up the newspaper and started reading. "'Early this month, General Crook went to Fort Robinson to attend a council meeting. On the way there, a native named Woman's Dress told the General that Crazy Horse intended to shake his hand and then stab him to death. Upon hearing this, General Crook ordered Crazy Horse's arrest.

"'At that point, Crazy Horse was still at the Spotted Tail Agency, not far from Fort Robinson. After Jesse Lee, the agent for Spotted Tail, explained what Woman's Dress had said, Crazy Horse denied he ever had any intention of killing General Crook. Agent Lee told him he understood this, but General Bradley insisted that Crazy Horse come to Fort Robinson and explain everything to him.

"'Agent Lee finally convinced Crazy Horse to return to Fort Robinson. Shortly after he arrived there, Crazy Horse realized he was being taken to a jail cell rather than actually meeting with the camp commander. At that point, he drew his knife and an infantry guard bayoneted him. He died shortly afterwards.'

"I expect more details will come out in the next few weeks, but none of it will change what happened. As for the rest of the evening, Chef has fixed a fine supper, and none of you needs to head back out to the range tonight. It's a beautiful evening to watch the moonrise.

"One more thing. When we were in town, one of the store owners told us that rustlers are stealing cattle and horses on the range. We'll need to be vigilant. Don't ever ride off alone."

Later that evening, Sanborn and Martin were the last ones remaining at the campfire. Sanborn glanced at Martin while he smothered the coals. "What do you think about Crazy Horse?"

"I know I can be honest with you. In some ways I regard him as a hero. He took risks to defend his people that I doubt I could ever have taken. He, along with Lakota leaders like Red Cloud and Sitting Bull, fought decisive battles against the U.S. Army, forcing them to abandon army forts in Montana and Wyoming. After that, each time a treaty was broken, he continued to fight for his people. I'm not sure I could have repeatedly risked my life the way he did, knowing the odds were stacked against me."

"I understand what you're saying, but here we are, building new lives for ourselves on land they once controlled. If gold hadn't been discovered here, things would have been very different."

A couple of weeks later, Sanborn waved to Martin when he came in from the range. "Yesterday I went into Spearfish to handle some legal business. There's a lawyer I've met with several times. His name is Adam Cranston. He's straightforward and, from what I can tell, a very decent man. When I mentioned your intention to practice law, he said he'd like to talk to you. When you're in town again, you should stop by his office. I think he'd like to find a good assistant."

"Thank you for telling him about me."

"Mind you, I'm in no rush for you to leave the ranch. All of you cowboys work hard and get along well."

Martin nodded his head. "Yes, we do. I'm thankful to be working on your ranch."

Practicing law in Spearfish would be an answer to his prayers. He might make a better living in Deadwood, but the town was too rough for his liking. He'd heard the early days of Spearfish were as wild as the pioneer days of Deadwood, but there were a few differences. Besides Deadwood's girlie houses, gambling dens, and twenty-five saloons, its Chinatown was filled with opium dens. He just didn't want to live in a town that wild. He slept soundly that night, blanketed by a burgeoning confidence. His desire to practice law was condensing into reality.

In late October, Sanborn asked Martin and one of the younger cowboys to take a wagon into Spearfish and get some supplies. "I know the weather's beautiful, but I'm taking no chances. A winter storm could strike early and with little warning. There's a reason that mound of hay bales is already stacked on the south side of the barn."

Before they headed back to the ranch that afternoon, Martin stopped by Cranston's law office. When he walked into the office, Martin introduced himself to the secretary.

"Mr. Cranston is with a client, but it shouldn't be much

longer. He's been hoping to talk to you. Could you wait for a bit?"

A short while later, Cranston invited Martin into his office. "I've been looking forward to meeting you. Andrew Sanborn speaks highly of you. Just how long have you been reading the law?"

"I arrived in Cheyenne in the summer of 1868 and started working on a cattle ranch. That winter, I read most of Stephen's first law volume. It helped pass those long winter evenings. Then, over the next few years, I finished reading the *Commentaries* and occasionally did some minor legal work for a Cheyenne law firm."

The conversation was cordial, but Martin didn't want to overstay his welcome. As he was getting up to leave, Cranston said, "What would you think about coming to work for me in February or March?"

"I'd like that very much. Also, I'm wondering if you could advise me about purchasing a small plot of land." After Martin explained where the lot was, Cranston said it should be no problem to arrange that.

"Stop by my office when you're in town again. I'll manage the purchase of that plat for you." Cranston extended his hand and they shook on it.

Near the end of October, Martin was out on the range when he saw White Wolf in the distance riding toward him. He hadn't seen him in more than a month. There was no need for Martin to flick the reins. Blaze was already heading toward him.

When they reached the stream where they usually met, both dismounted and let their horses wander in the brush. Martin pulled an envelope from his inner jacket pocket.

"In three moons I will leave the ranch and move to Spearfish. Until then, we meet here. After that, I will work for a lawyer in town." Martin handed White Wolf a map of Spearfish that he'd drawn. "Here is where I'll build a log cabin. It's close to Spearfish, near a small stream. After four moons, come to the cabin to find me." He hoped White Wolf had understood most of what he'd said. He watched White Wolf study the map. "Do you understand where the cabin will be?"

White Wolf nodded his head.

"After the cabin is built, if you hunt near there, you stay with me."

White Wolf nodded again.

Martin reached into his saddlebag and pulled out some hardtack and dried meat for them to eat.

In November, Martin was riding along the periphery of Sanborn's ranch, checking the location of the cattle, when suddenly the sky darkened. The wind quickly shifted to the northwest and the temperature dropped. When the cattle started massing, Martin knew he had to head back to the ranch. Within minutes, he was blinded by the snow and had lost all sense of direction. Even Blaze seemed confused, something Martin had never witnessed. For all he knew, they might be heading away from the ranch. Then Blaze neighed and Martin glanced ahead. A vague, dark shape appeared and disappeared in the thickly falling snow. Blaze immediately started following it. The shape, disappearing and reappearing, stayed ahead of them all the way back to the ranch.

Once Blaze was in the stable and fed, Martin pounded on the cabin door. Sanborn opened the door and pulled Martin inside. "We've been concerned about you."

"Is everyone else here?"

"Yes. I'll have Cook fix you some supper. Is Blaze all right?"

Martin nodded. "I've never been caught in a blizzard like this. I wasn't sure if we were heading in the right direction.

Then something strange happened. Blaze saw it first. A dark shape kept appearing and disappearing in front of us, and Blaze followed it all the way back to the ranch."

"What do you think it was?"

"It sounds far-fetched, but I felt that White Wolf was guiding us. I know that seems impossible. What do you think?" Martin looked at Sanborn.

"The rational part of my mind says it isn't possible. The intuitive part isn't so sure about that. Spirit can act in mysterious ways."

Later that week, a letter arrived from James. They had promised to exchange letters on a monthly basis, even if there wasn't much news. After he finished reading James's latest letter, Martin took a deep breath and read it again.

Dear Martin,

Last week Doc Matheson came into the store and motioned that he'd like to talk. When I finished with a customer, we went to the back of the shop.

He asked about you and looked relieved when I told him that Sanborn runs a respectable ranching operation. He also asked about your decision to leave his ranch. I said it was because of his wife's nephew and mentioned that Jake had warned you to watch your back when Jed was around. I told him about Jed aiming a gun at you and lowering it only when another cowboy rode up.

He said he'd never trusted Jed from the first day he landed on the ranch. He only did it as a favor to his wife. Last month he forced Jed to leave because he was provoking fights with other cowboys. Doc wishes he'd done it sooner because he thinks you might still be around. I can tell he misses you and would appreciate getting a letter from you. One more thing. He's planning to send your buffalo hide to you on one of the stagecoach runs to Spearfish.

I hope someday you'll come to Cheyenne for a visit. Doc

would very much like to see you and so would I. Also, I have met a lovely young schoolteacher. She just might be the woman I've been dreaming would come into my life.

With brotherly love,

James

In early December, Martin picked up a large package at the post office with Doc Matheson's return address on it. Before he went to bed that night, he wrote Doc a letter.

Dear Doc,

Earlier this month, James sent a letter relating his conversation with you. Before I left Cheyenne, I told James that if it weren't for the incidents with Jed, I would never have left your ranch until I could practice law. He wrote he conveyed that to you. Over the years I worked for you, I learned how a good ranch should be run. I also learned about legal issues related to ranching. It will all come in handy when I find work in a law office.

Thank you for sending the buffalo hide. I'm grateful to have its protection over the winter. I often think about our conversations on your front porch. Someday I'll get back to Cheyenne to visit James and hope to see you then.

With my best regards,

Martin

Ever since Doc sent the buffalo hide, Martin had wanted to give it to White Wolf. An article in *The Black Hills Pioneer* reported that the southern herd of bison, which once numbered around five million, no longer existed. This was done by design through U.S. government policy. It happened in less than twenty years and was devastating for the tribes. The Lakota had long relied on the buffalo for food, clothing, and shelter.

The article also reported that the Powder River country and the Black Hills were taken from them. The Lakota tribes used to spend their winters in those areas, near rivers with protective bluffs and thick cottonwood groves. The land on the Pine Ridge Reservation wasn't arable and lacked water. The article said the majority of the Lakota had no horses and that it was impossible for them to feed and clothe themselves. It also stated that government rations weren't adequate. Martin wondered how the tribes could survive.

Several times a week, he checked the creek where he usually met White Wolf, but found no tracks. One day, just as he was about to leave the creek, he saw White Wolf riding toward him. He took a deep breath and slowly released it. He'd been concerned he might never see him again.

"White Wolf, it's good to see you. I have something back at the ranch to give you. Will you ride there with me?"

White Wolf nodded and they headed to the ranch.

Sanborn was stacking firewood when they arrived. Martin introduced him to White Wolf, then went into the bunkhouse to get the buffalo hide. He caught a glimpse of Sanborn trying to talk to White Wolf. Martin's esteem for Sanborn went up another notch.

When Martin came out with the buffalo hide, White Wolf nodded his head in thanks. Sanborn helped them rig a travois from a couple of branches.

Martin decided to ride with White Wolf for a few miles to make sure the travois held up. "White Wolf, I've been waiting to see you. There's something I want to ask you."

White Wolf looked at him.

"In November, Blaze and I were caught in a snowstorm. We were lost and couldn't see our way back to Sanborn's ranch. Then something happened. Blaze shook his head and whinnied. We saw a dark shape ahead of us. Sometimes the snow covered it but then it would come back. It led us to the ranch, then disappeared. I felt your spirit was leading us. Is this so?"

"It could be my spirit traveled and did this."

After a couple of miles, Martin halted Blaze. "In one more moon, I will be in Spearfish. In three moons my cabin will be built."

"I see you after winter."

Martin waited until White Wolf disappeared over a hill, then rode back to the ranch.

In early January, Martin arranged for a wire transfer from his Cheyenne bank to purchase the lot for his cabin. After that, he went to Cranston's office to discuss when he could start working for him.

"Martin, I could use your assistance as soon as possible. Spearfish now has over 150 residents, not including the number of ranchers and farmers living nearby."

"I just purchased a lot on the edge of town. As soon as I can arrange it, I'll have a log cabin and stable built there. Until then, I'll rent a room above one of the stores on main street. Sanborn is in full support of my doing this. I could start next week."

Cranston extended his hand. "Let's shake on that. I look forward to working with you."

"I feel the same. Thank you for this opportunity. I promise you won't regret it. I do have one question, though. It's about the cattle rustling and horse stealing that's occurring in the Northern Hills. Spearfish, Deadwood, and the smaller communities are all affected by it. The bands of rustlers are getting very bold and are too big a problem for the local law officials to handle alone.

"I'm sure you're aware that stockmen have formed a vigilante group to capture and punish these rustlers. Unless there's legal work that requires urgent attention, I'd like to ride with them when they're tracking down rustlers and horse thieves."

"That's fine with me, Martin. Those lawbreakers need to be punished. I'm too old to go riding with you. I hope there won't be much blood spilled."

"So far the bloodshed has been minimal. It might take a while, but once the rustlers realize the vigilantes are serious about capturing and punishing them, things should settle down."

When Martin worked on the range, the days raced by. He hadn't expected this would also occur in a law office, but Cranston's backlog of work for Martin made the days pass quickly. Cranston treated him with respect, always introducing his clients to Martin, making it clear that he valued his work. At noon, he and Cranston usually went to one of the cafés for dinner.

Martin adapted to town life fairly quickly, but he missed the freedom of the open range. He exercised Blaze each day and took him for long rides on Sundays, usually ending up at Sanborn's ranch, sometimes spending the night. The bond of their friendship was growing deeper, as it had with Doc Matheson. It was a gift, and he gave thanks for it.

In late March, near the end of a workday, Cranston drew down the shade on the front door and came over to Martin's desk. "How about joining me for supper tonight? We could go to that café you like so much."

"Yes, I'd appreciate it."

Cranston requested a small table in the back of the restaurant. "It should be less noisy back here. Feel free to order whatever you'd like. Supper's on me."

After they ordered, Cranston continued, "Between your experience at the ranch outside Cheyenne and then working for Sanborn, you learned a lot about the cattle industry. My clients tell me you also understand farming and are good at resolving issues between ranchers and farmers. They think you're fair, even if they don't always like the compromises you propose. They understand you're looking for an equitable resolution. People will trust you if they know you can't be bought."

Martin looked down for a moment. Praise rarely occurred in his family. "Thank you. I was fortunate to work for two good ranchers. And I've learned a lot working for you these past months."

"Well, I'm glad you think that. It also helps that you spend part of your evenings researching the law. I see you taking law texts home many evenings. Besides knowledge, having a reputation for fairness is worth its weight in gold. Of course, I have no idea how one would actually estimate that."

"Perhaps you could develop a formula for that."

Cranston smiled. "I'll think about it."

6

MARTIN'S CABIN AND STABLE WERE COMPLETED IN LATE May 1878. The cabin was basic but could easily be expanded if he ever had a family. After he settled into the cabin, he noticed a crow's nest in a pine tree near the house. He didn't admit it to anyone, but he liked having a neighbor. The crow always squawked hello when Martin came home from work, and Martin left a handful of nuts or seeds at the base of the tree each day. In return, the crow sometimes left little gifts, like pieces of mica, at the front doorstep.

Whenever White Wolf appeared, the crow announced his arrival in a special voice, not his usual raucous cry. White Wolf always stopped beneath the pine tree to greet the crow. After watching this several times, Martin asked White Wolf what he said to the crow.

"*Kangí* means 'crow.' I greet my crow brother. He is sign of good luck for you. Watch him closely. He is smart. Sometimes he is a messenger. Sometimes he is a trickster."

"Do you mean something bad?"

"No, he likes to play tricks." White Wolf smiled to himself.

"You mean just to amuse himself?"

White Wolf nodded. "Also, crow cleans the land, eating dead prey that man will not eat."

"What other things do you know about crows?"

"*Kangí* is a shape-shifter. He can live in bird nature and in spirit. When a crow appears to you, it can mean you must decide whether to follow the path you are taking or choose a different one."

On a Saturday in mid-June, Martin rode Blaze to his favorite fishing spot. White Wolf had taught him what to look for when he was out alone. Broken branches could mean that prey was nearby. He also taught Martin how to read tracks that were barely visible in the ground. White Wolf never used a compass and never got lost. He had a sense of where he was at all times.

When Martin and Blaze reached Spearfish Creek, he noticed moccasin and horse tracks. He followed the tracks and found White Wolf leaning on a stick. Martin dismounted, ran over to him, and helped him sit on a log. There was a cut on his lower leg.

Martin walked back to his saddlebag and returned with a small jar wrapped in cloth. "This is honey. I'll wash that wound, then spread honey over it. It will help heal that cut and keep it from getting infected." Martin knew that White Wolf didn't understand everything he'd said but felt sure he understood the gist of it.

White Wolf winced when Martin rinsed the wound, then watched attentively as he spread honey over it with the cloth. Martin left the cloth on the wound, then took his bandana and tied it over the cloth, making sure it was tight.

They fished for several hours, sitting in the silence of comfortable friendship. Midafternoon, Martin shared some hardtack and dried beef with White Wolf. "Let's leave soon. You should stay at my cabin tonight so I can look at your leg in the morning."

White Wolf shook his head.

"Please. We can eat these fish for supper. I want to make sure you're all right. I bought another buffalo hide so you can sleep on the porch."

White Wolf finally nodded.

Martin knew that White Wolf didn't like being inside the cabin. The only time he'd invited White Wolf to come inside, White Wolf refused and remained standing at the front door. With this in mind, Martin hauled the buffalo hide out to the front porch for them to sit on, then went back inside to fry the fish and some potatoes.

After they finished eating, Martin pointed to White Wolf's leg. "I'd like to look at that cut." White Wolf nodded, and Martin removed the cloth. "It looks good. I'm going to clean it and put a fresh bandage over it. I'll check it again in the morning. Do you live far from here?"

"Near Wounded Knee Creek."

"I have another question. Did you choose your name?"

White Wolf nodded. "I was young boy, hunting with bow. I shoot two pheasants but did not mark trail. I was lost. I ask spirit to guide me. My mind sees gulley with small trees. I remember I was there long time ago, different life. Then white wolf comes out from gulley and nods for me to follow. He leads me back to camp. After that I call myself White Wolf. One must honor visions."

Early the next morning, Martin went to the front porch, hoping to find White Wolf, but he was gone. He poured himself a second cup of coffee and watched the day come to life, still thinking about White Wolf's comments. Sanborn had told him the Lakota didn't fear physical death. They believed in a spirit world called *Wakan Tanka*. It was a beautiful day to ride over to his ranch and explore the subject.

While Martin was riding, he thought about what the Sauk and Meskwaki had experienced in Iowa. It was a stark contrast to what the western tribes had gone through and were still going through. His high school teacher told him the Sauk and Meskwaki moved into Iowa in the 1700s, forced west by European settlement in the eastern states. In 1845, through a series of government demands, the tribes lost their lands in Iowa and were forced to move to Kansas. But not all of them left. Some resisted and went into hiding. Nine years later, the State of Iowa enacted a law that allowed the tribes to reside in Iowa and purchase eighty acres in Tama County.

Then, in 1867, the U.S. government allowed the Sauk and Meskwaki living in Iowa to receive federal annuity payments. His teacher stressed that it gave the tribes a unique identity. Their privately purchased property was now considered a sovereign nation. The State of Iowa also recognized the new status. Tribal members who had moved to Kansas started returning to the settlement. No other tribes in the country had this designation. It was a stark contrast to the Lakota's loss of the Black Hills.

That same year, the Sauk and Meskwaki traded 130 trees for funds to purchase another forty acres, bringing their settlement to 3,000 acres. Between annuity payments and income from trapping, they survived. The settlement lay about eighty miles north of Martin's family farm. At the time, Martin didn't think much about it and certainly didn't appreciate its unique legal status. His family had to focus on surviving and establishing a homestead.

When he saw Blaze approaching, Sanborn's horse whinnied from a paddock and Blaze responded. After he left Blaze in the paddock, Martin walked over to Sanborn.

"This is a nice surprise. What brings you here? Not that you aren't welcome just to ride over for a visit. It's a beautiful day."

"Yes, it is. Blaze likes these long rides, and so do I. But today I have another reason for coming here. You once said the Lakota believe in past lives. At the time, I wasn't familiar with the concept and wasn't sure what to think. Now I'm ready to hear what you have to say about it."

"This will be an interesting conversation. Let's sit on the front porch. What caused your sudden interest in this?"

"Yesterday I went fishing in Spearfish Creek and just happened to come across White Wolf. He'd cut his leg and was limping. I always carry some honey in my saddlebag to treat wounds, so I cleaned the cut, applied some honey, and wrapped a cloth around it. After that, we fished for a couple of hours, and I insisted that he spend the night at my place so I could check the cut in the morning.

"I fried some fish for dinner and put a fresh bandage on the cut. I asked him where he lived, and he said near Wounded Knee Creek. Then I asked him how he chose his name. And that is the reason I came here today. This is what he told me.

"When he was young, maybe fifteen, he was riding his horse, tracking a deer. The deer was clever, not easy to track. White Wolf rode into territory he didn't know. The tracks ended where the deer crossed a stream, so he rode across the stream. Once he got to the other side, he couldn't find any tracks. He rode for a while, then gave up the hunt and turned around.

"When he got back to the stream, he couldn't find the exact place he'd crossed. Nothing looked familiar. It was impossible for him to retrace his tracks. Then he dismounted and stretched out on the grasses. When he shut his eyes, he saw an image of the stream with trees growing beside it. The trees were young, not old and big. The path of the stream was different. He said the memory came from a different lifetime. Not this one.

"I asked him what he meant by a different lifetime. His response is why I'm here. He said the Lakota believe that spirit lives on after the body is gone. The body drops like a robe, but the spirit doesn't die. The memory of the stream came from an earlier lifetime. When he stood up and looked across the riverbank, a white wolf was standing near some trees. It stared at him, then called for him to follow. After an hour or so, the wolf led him back to his original trail. That's the reason he chose the name White Wolf. What do you think about this?"

"Well, Martin. Just how honest do you want me to be?"

"I'd like you to be completely honest. I'm intrigued by it."

"First of all, I've been hearing about the afterlife and spirits since I was a young boy. I grew up in St. Louis at a time when there was an active fur trade with natives in the Far West. One of my uncles was a trader and hired me to work in his shop. When hunters and trappers returned to St. Louis with their furs and buffalo hides, I heard lots of stories about the West. It made me want to see the world they talked about.

"One of the trappers told me the Lakota are brave because they don't fear death. They believe in spirits, afterlives, and reincarnation. They think the natural and supernatural worlds are linked, that the natural world is infused with spirit. It's a lot to comprehend, isn't it?"

"Yes, it is. I'd like to read about it."

Sanborn smiled. "I've always thought you had a curious mind. Many people feel threatened by beliefs that are different from the ones they were raised with. I have a book of essays written by Ralph Waldo Emerson. I'd be glad to loan it to you. It would be a good start for you."

"Thank you. I expect we'll have a good discussion when I finish it."

On a beautiful Saturday in late September, Martin was preparing a supper of hardtack and beans. He'd left the front door and windows open all day to air out the cabin. When Blaze whinnied, he glanced out the window and saw White Wolf riding toward them. Martin waved to him and hauled the buffalo skin to the front porch, pleased to have White Wolf's company for dinner.

After they finished eating, Martin said, "I also had a vision to change my name."

White Wolf raised his eyebrows and nodded for Martin to continue.

Martin went inside and came back with a map. After spreading it out close to White Wolf, he pointed to various locations. "Here are the territories of Montana, Wyoming, Dakota, Nebraska. This is Paha Sapa, Black Hills. Here is the Missouri River. I come from here, the state of Iowa. This is the Mississippi River. Here is Chicago where big trains take cattle to sell. After I sold my family's cattle in Chicago, I was attacked. The money was stolen. I could not return home without the money, so I climbed into a railroad car going to Wyoming. I worked on a cattle ranch until I came here."

White Wolf pointed to the map. "White River. I live near here."

Martin looked. "Near the Badlands on the Pine Ridge Reservation."

White Wolf nodded. "Not good land to farm. Before white men take our land, we hunted for buffalo in fall. In winter we lived near rivers. Bluffs and cottonwoods protected us. The generals destroyed our world. Their world is built on the carcasses of tribes and buffalo and destruction of nature. Now they have gold, but that will not be enough. I fear they will take our children."

They alternated between silence and periods of talk until dusk descended. Then Martin went into the cabin. White Wolf slept on the buffalo hide with his rifle at his side. At about one o'clock in the morning, White Wolf's horse pawed the ground and snorted.

Hearing the horse, Martin pulled on a pair of Levis, grabbed his rifle, and ran out to the porch. White Wolf was walking quietly toward his horse, prepared to fire his rifle.

Martin ran up behind him. "What do you think it is?"

"Bear." White Wolf grabbed his horse's rein and tried to settle him.

Martin heard a crunching sound and looked at White Wolf. White Wolf nodded and pointed to bushes near the side of the cabin. The new moon cast just enough light for Martin to see a dark shape shifting. Surely the bear smelled them. Martin heard a sharp crack from White Wolf's rifle, then a second one. "Are you sure it's dead?"

White Wolf nodded. "I take bear with me."

"We'll use my wagon and take the bear partway to your camp. Then you use the travois. We leave at sunrise." Martin was immensely impressed with White Wolf's ability at tracking prey. He read tracks in the ground that were barely visible.

Just before dawn, they loaded the bear and travois into the wagon. White Wolf tied his horse to the wagon and rode with Martin. They didn't talk much, but White Wolf mentioned there were shortages of food, clothing, blankets, and shelter on the reservation. At midday, he looked up at the sun. "We stop here."

After they secured the bear on the travois, White Wolf headed to the reservation. Martin stayed put, wanting to make sure the travois would hold up. When White Wolf reached the edge of a gulch, he turned and waved. Martin waved back, then headed home. While he was riding, a cloak of sadness draped itself around him. Until then, native societies had enforced tribal law and kept the peace, but that was now outlawed. Under recent legislation, Indian agents could hire police for law enforcement on the reservations.

And that wasn't all. The U.S. government had further violated its treaties by seizing tribal lands and releasing them for settlement to non-natives. White Wolf had told Martin that tribes who were traditional enemies were now forced to live together on reservations that were far too small for the number of natives forced to live on them.

In mid-October, Martin was chopping wood when he spotted White Wolf in the distance. He stood up and waved to him. He didn't like the way White Wolf looked, half bent over his horse. Something wasn't right.

Martin went inside and brought back some biscuits and dried meat for him. White Wolf tethered his horse near Blaze, then walked over to the front porch. Martin had never seen him look so sad.

Martin spread a blanket on the porch and gestured for White Wolf to sit down. "I see your sadness. What has happened?"

"They open schoolhouse at Pine Ridge Indian Agency in September. My nephew goes there. On first day they cut off hair of students. We only do this if family member dies. They make them wear uniforms and march for long time. If our children speak our language, the teachers slap them and force lye soap into their mouth. They make them scrub floors on hands and knees every morning, wash laundry, do housekeeping, kitchen work, and farm chores." White Wolf looked away, trying not to cry.

"This makes me furious. It's much worse than I feared it would be. It's evil." Martin had read the goal of the schools was to weaken students' bonds to tribe and family and take their language away. They wanted to force native students to assume a white, English-speaking, Christian culture but still not treat them as equals.

In late May 1880, Martin picked up a copy of *The Black Hills Pioneer*, Deadwood's newspaper. The front page carried an article about the Carlisle Indian Industrial School, which had been established in Pennsylvania the previous fall. The founder, Captain Richard Henry Pratt, explained the school's philosophy in this way: "A great general has said that the only good Indian is a dead one, and that high sanction of his destruction had been an enormous factor in promoting Indian massacres. In a sense, I agree with the sentiment, but only in this: that all the Indian there is in the race should be dead. Kill the Indian in him, and save the man."

Martin read the article very carefully. Basically, the stated goal of the Carlisle program was the assimilation of native children into white society. They were forbidden to speak their native languages and were beaten if they did. The school tried to make them shed all tribal ways. Students were not allowed to return to their families in the summer. Instead, they were placed with white families. Of Carlisle's original first-year class of 136 students, six died and fifteen were sent home to die.

The article also stated that dozens of Christian missionary boarding schools were being established with the same goal of assimilating native children into the white culture. An added incentive for the establishment of these schools was the U.S. government's payment per student, with no controls on how the money was spent. The students were mainly trained to do menial labor, and their basic needs were often neglected.

By the time he finished reading the article, Martin was furious. No wonder White Wolf looked wounded whenever Martin saw him. The article triggered the memory of a conversation with James shortly after they'd met. James had explained that he joined the Union Army because he believed that all humans are God's children, no matter the color of their skin.

Martin agreed completely with James. At many of the schools, if native children died, their bodies were thrown into unmarked graves without notifying their families. No matter how long it took, he hoped one day there would be a reckoning for those who instituted these vile policies.

Now in his third year of law practice, Martin finally trusted he could make a decent livelihood in Spearfish. The town was growing slowly but steadily, and farmers and ranchers were establishing footholds. He and Cranston never lacked for work.

Several weekends in May, Martin helped with the spring roundup on Sanborn's ranch. Rounding up cattle on the open range meant working sixteen- to eighteen-hour days. The calves were branded, the herd counted, and those not going to market released back onto the range. It was hard work, but he and Blaze liked being part of it. While it was a nice change of pace, he was thankful he didn't have to work full-time as a cowboy.

Martin was usually the first one in the office but, when he came to work on Monday, he was surprised to find Cranston waiting for him.

"Good morning, Martin. Over the weekend I was thinking about the case that involves an incident in Deadwood. I'd like you to go there and introduce yourself to Karl Johnson, the editor of *The Black Hills Pioneer*. He's a decent man and a good resource for background information. Let's make a list of concerns we have and, if the weather holds, you could go there sometime this week."

"I'd be glad to do that. I have some errands I could tend to while I'm there."

Early the next morning, Martin hitched Blaze to his two-wheeled cart and headed to Deadwood. The sunrise was striking, with delicate wisps of cirrus clouds rising above the Black Hills. He suddenly felt this was going to be a significant day for him.

Martin tied Blaze to a hitching post outside the newspaper office, then went in and introduced himself to Johnson.

Johnson shook Martin's hand and said, "I'd be pleased to answer any questions you have about the Deadwood case."

Martin was amazed how quickly the hour passed. He didn't want to overstay his welcome. He wanted to have more discussions like this in the future. "Thank you for your time, your advice, and your opinions. It was a pleasure to meet you."

"It was a pleasure to meet you too. Stop by anytime you're in Deadwood. I hope you'll be able to meet my partner Laughlin the next time you're here."

Martin nodded. "Thank you."

He definitely wanted to take Johnson up on his offer. Their conversation was enlightening and wide-ranging. While he was riding down Main Street, he saw a striking young woman step off a stagecoach. She looked lost and afraid. Martin saw one of the bar owners heading her way and knew exactly what he had in mind.

He tied Blaze to a hitching post and walked quickly to the young woman. "Excuse me, miss. The man heading your way owns the Real Gem Saloon. Did he pay for your fare on the stagecoach?"

"No. I paid my way here. I read an advertisement about the saloon. I don't have much money left." She glanced at the bar owner and looked frightened.

"I'm sure he will try to hire you. He'll tell you that you will only have to dance with customers, but you can't trust him. I live in Spearfish, not far from here. I'm a lawyer. An Episcopal minister and his wife are friends of mine. I'm quite sure they would take you into their home until you could find work and safe lodging. I'm willing to cover any expenses you might have. Someone once rescued me, and I'm now in a position to do the same. You'd have no obligation to me. By the way, my name is Martin Handshoe."

"Why would you help me?"

"Because I saw the look on your face when he started walking toward you. He's rough, and you sensed that. I don't know what you're escaping from, but you don't have to do this."

"Why did you come to the Black Hills?"

"I grew up in Iowa, one of four sons, too many sons for one farm. Besides, from the time I was young, I knew I didn't want to work the land. I wanted to be a lawyer. So I took a train to Wyoming and worked on a ranch for three years. I studied my law texts over the long winters and did some minor work for a law firm in Cheyenne.

"Three years ago, I worked a cattle drive to Spearfish, hoping to have a better chance of practicing law there. Nine months later, I moved to town and started working for a small law firm. It's a nice town, not quite as wild as Deadwood. I think it would be a safe place for you."

She took another look at the owner of the bar. "I'll go with you if you cross your heart that you'll keep your word to me."

Martin crossed his heart with his thumb. "I promise to honor my word."

He helped her into the cart, and they headed out of Deadwood. She sat as far away from him as she possibly could. "Do you have a habit of rescuing women from saloon work?"

Martin laughed. "No, this is the first time. That's why I'm struggling with what to say to you. Most women who come to Deadwood have a good idea of the life they will lead. Many want to be dance girls but end up being prostitutes. You don't look like that kind of woman. What's your name?"

"My name is Adrianna Ennis."

"Adrianna's a beautiful name. What kind of name is Ennis?"

"My father was Irish, and my mother was Scottish."

"So that explains your red hair." He'd never seen such beautiful red hair—long, wavy, thick. "What do you mean 'was'? Have they passed on?"

"I'm from Missouri. Early this year, my parents died in a flu epidemic, so I went to live with my sister's family near Sioux Falls. She has two children. From the very start, I didn't trust her husband. This week he tried to trap me in the barn when I was collecting chicken eggs. I ran into the house and begged my sister to help me escape.

"That night she gave me some money and said I should be able to find work in the Black Hills. I left before daybreak, walked into town, and took the first stagecoach heading west. How did you come by that scar near your eye?"

"A long time ago I took some cattle to market. After I made the sale and was heading back to the railroad station, a couple of men attacked me and robbed me. I resisted them and ended up with this scar."

Martin quickly changed the direction of the conversation. If she asked anything else about him, he'd tell her about working on the ranch in Wyoming and his pursuit of reading the law. Ever since fleeing from the Chicago stockyards, his storyline had always been that four brothers were too many brothers for one farm, that he decided to head West so he could make a living and pursue his legal career.

"We're about to enter the Spearfish Creek Canyon. I always feel a sense of reverence when I ride through it. There's a different energy here, probably because of the beautiful stream and the ancient boulders. I have a Lakota friend, White Wolf. Sometimes we come here to fish. The Lakota are very good with spearing fish. That's how the river got its name."

"I've never seen anything like this. It's so beautiful."

Martin looked at Adrianna, thinking he could say the same about her.

It was midafternoon when they arrived in Spearfish. Martin showed Adrianna the town's main street, pointed out the law office where he worked, and then went to the McGranes' house. "Please stay here while I explain your situation to the McGranes. It will just take a minute."

Rebekah McGrane opened the front door before Martin had a chance to knock. "I just happened to look out the front window and see you. If you're looking for David, he's attending a meeting."

"Well, perhaps it's better if I talk to you first anyway. I

went to Deadwood this morning to meet with the editor of the newspaper. After the meeting, I was on my way out of town when I saw a young woman stepping out of a stage-coach—the young lady who's sitting in my cart."

Rebekah looked and smiled at Adrianna.

"That's Adrianna. She just escaped from a desperate situation. When her parents passed away this year, she was forced to live with her sister's family near Sioux Falls. The problem was her brother-in-law was becoming aggressive with her. She needed to escape before something bad happened. Her sister gave her some money to get as far as Deadwood. This is very bold to ask, but I was wondering if you and the reverend could shelter her for a bit. I will gladly pay for her to stay with you."

"She looks frightened, doesn't she?"

"Yes, ma'am. That was the first thing I noticed."

"Well, please invite her inside so we can meet."

"Welcome, Adrianna. It's a pleasure to meet you. Let's go into the sitting room. After I make some tea, we'll sort out your situation."

Martin sat beside Adrianna on the sofa. "You will be safe here. They're very kind people."

She blinked back tears. "I can't thank you enough."

While they drank tea and nibbled on cookies, Rebekah took stock of Adrianna's situation. "Here's what I think we should do. You're welcome to stay with us while you establish a new life for yourself. I expect you're exhausted from that long ride in the stagecoach.

"There's a bedroom on the first floor that we save for com-pany. That would be your room if you decide to stay with us. After we finish our tea, I think you should go there and rest for a while. Your presence in our home would be a wonderful surprise for my husband David. We seldom see our daughters and miss them very much. Martin, I'll serve supper at six o'clock."

7

FOR THE NEXT THREE MONTHS, MARTIN SAW ADRIANNA every day. Thanks to Rebekah's support, Adrianna's talent as a seamstress was becoming recognized in the community. Her increasing self-confidence sparkled like a star in the night sky. Martin loved seeing her blossom. Sometimes they shared supper with the McGranes, but usually they ate at a restaurant on Main Street.

"How was your day today?"

"It was busy. Most of the morning I worked on a quilt with Rebekah. In the afternoon, a mother and daughter stopped by and asked me to make dresses for them. They already had the fabric but wanted me to design the dresses."

"Congratulations. People are not only recognizing your talent as a seamstress but also as a designer."

"My grandmother was an excellent seamstress. I owe all my sewing skills to her. I spent many an afternoon at her side. It's interesting to work with Rebekah on the quilt design. I'm learning a lot, and I'm thankful for her companionship."

"I'm sure she feels the same way about working with you."

"Why is it you never go to bars?"

"Well, that's certainly changing the subject! The church my family attended forbade any use of alcohol. There was never any alcohol in our home, and we were forbidden from going to bars. After I arrived in Wyoming, I watched what happens in bars. Men drink too much, get into fights, and sometimes even kill each other. Also, I don't like to hear them brag about what they do with the women they take upstairs to the rooms above the bars. It has nothing to do with loving someone."

"Rebekah said that sometimes people have no way to pay you, but you represent them anyway. She said you're an honorable man."

"It was kind of her to say that." Martin seldom went to church because the church he attended as a child was harsh and judgmental. He was glad to know Rebekah had some respect for him even though he rarely set foot inside their church. She'd once asked him about his religious upbringing and, after he explained, just nodded her head.

"Do you like to dance?"

"I don't know how to dance. The church I attended was very strict about that kind of thing. Why do you ask?"

"Rebekah said there's going to be a wedding dance Saturday night, and we're welcome to attend. Where I grew up in Missouri, it was common for people to have a wedding dance when they got married."

"Would you like to go to the wedding dance?"

"Yes. I could teach you to dance a waltz step. It isn't difficult."

"All right. Tomorrow night we'll have supper at my house, and you may try to teach me to dance."

The next evening, Adrianna hummed waltz melodies and taught Martin to dance. "You're a very good student. Tomorrow night people will think you've been dancing for years."

With each step, his insecurities slowly dissolved. "I like holding you in my arms."

"And I like being held in your arms."

At just that moment, he tripped and they fell into each other's arms, which turned into an embrace and a long kiss.

Still holding her close, Martin said, "I've wanted to do that for a long time."

"Me too."

"Let's go sit on the front porch and watch the stars come out. By accident or by divine providence, you're the most wonderful thing that has ever happened to me."

Adrianna placed her hand on top of Martin's. "We're tested when bad things happen. Being a good person doesn't mean life will protect you. Circumstances forced both of us to leave our families. Perhaps fate meant for us to find each other. Anyway, I'd like to believe that. Do you believe in kismet?" Adrianna gently touched the scar near Martin's eye.

"Do you mean fate?" Martin took her hand and kissed it.

"Yes. I believe destiny had a hand in our meeting each other."

"I'm not sure if things happen accidentally or through some grand design."

Blaze was foraging nearby, periodically looking over at them and nickering. The crow was up in his tree, shouting at them from time to time.

"Would you mind if I name the crow Ezekiel? He's always making pronouncements, like Ezekiel in the Old Testament. I'm not sure what he's saying, but I think he's trying to talk to us. I've noticed you treat him well."

"I like that idea. I think he'd like it too. Crows are very intelligent. In fact, I have something I'd like him to announce."

"What on earth are you thinking about?"

He knelt and reached for her hand. "Will you marry me?"

Blinking back tears, she managed to say, "Yes, Martin."

"Ezekiel, you may now announce our engagement."

Ezekiel responded enthusiastically, especially after they scattered handfuls of nuts on the ground.

"The day you rescued me in Deadwood, I was nervous about leaving with you. But then, when we passed along Spearfish Creek, a sense of peace came over me. From the tone of your voice and your kind words, I knew I could trust you. After we reached Spearfish and you left me with Rebekah, I felt a sense of safety I hadn't felt in years. I've never known anyone like you."

Martin pulled Adrianna toward him and held her close. "We were meant to be together. What would you think about getting married in early September? I know it's only a couple of weeks away."

"I would like that. I'm sure Rebekah will help me make a wedding dress, and I think Reverend McGrane would be pleased to marry us."

When Martin stopped by the next evening to take Adrianna to supper, Rebekah opened the door. "Please have supper with us tonight. David and I were so happy to learn of your engagement. Adrianna said it will be a very small wedding. We're wondering if you'd like to be married in our backyard. The weather is so beautiful now. We could discuss this over supper. Also, I told Adrianna I'd be pleased to make her wedding dress."

"Thank you. That would all be wonderful."

In mid-September, the day before their wedding, Martin went to the McGranes' home to collect Adrianna's belongings. After loading them in the wagon, he waved to them. "I'll bring her back later this afternoon."

When they arrived at the cabin, Martin helped Adrianna down from the wagon. "Before I bring your belongings inside, I have something to show you. Come inside and see what I have for you."

She followed him back to the bedroom.

"I had this wardrobe made for you. Now I'll bring your things in and you can arrange them as you see fit."

"Martin, it's perfect. Thank you. I've never had anything like this."

He noticed her blinking back tears. Her life hadn't been easy, but he had no doubt they'd create a beautiful life together. For a few moments he watched her carefully store some belongings. It seemed to be a significant event for her.

When she came out, Martin was sitting at the kitchen table, holding something in his hand.

"What are you looking at?"

"Please sit down. There's something I want to give you. It belonged to my mother's mother. I hope you'll wear it when we're married tomorrow. Open your hand."

She opened her hand and Martin laid Oma's necklace across her palm.

"What a beautiful gemstone. What kind of stone is this?"

"It's amber, and there's a story that goes along with it. Before my family sailed from Amsterdam, my Oma Magdalena gave the pendant to my mother Nellie. My mother regarded it as a talisman and wore it every day.

"In 1868, just before I left for the Chicago stockyards, she tucked an envelope into my coat pocket. Here's the note she wrote to me. Please read it aloud."

"'Martyn, my heart is heavy with concern that you're traveling to Chicago by yourself. I will not be at peace until you return home. I pray Oma Magdalena's pendant will protect you. Your mother, Nell.'" Adrianna looked at him, her eyes filled with questions.

"The day before I left for Chicago, I felt very uneasy. Clearly my mother also had a sense of foreboding about my traveling there alone. You know the rest of the story. After I was robbed, my family surely lost our farm. I think she senses I'm still alive. I wish you two could meet one day. Let's sit on the porch for a while. It's such a beautiful fall afternoon. I'll take you back to the McGranes' in an hour."

The next afternoon, Reverend McGrane married them in their backyard. Rebekah surprised Adrianna with a beautiful bouquet of flowers from her garden. The ceremony was intimate, with only a handful of friends attending, and the McGranes hosted a lovely reception. They were home by twilight and before long disappeared into the bedroom.

Martin, always an early riser, was pouring a second cup of coffee when Adrianna appeared the next morning. "Good morning, sleepyhead."

"Well, I think I have a very good reason for sleeping so late." She sat on Martin's lap and hugged him.

He folded his arms around her. "Before we have breakfast, I should check on Blaze."

"I'd like to go with you and say good morning to him."

Martin watched Blaze nuzzle Adrianna's extended hand. They'd liked each other from their first meeting. "How about going for a ride in the cart this afternoon? We could take a picnic to Spearfish Creek."

"Yes, that's a wonderful idea."

Until he'd met Adrianna, Martin was beginning to wonder if he would ever find a mate. Her presence in his life had triggered a depth of emotion he didn't know was possible.

The following week, Adrianna stayed home to clear an area for a garden. As soon as spring arrived, she intended to plant flowers and vegetables. When Martin came home late that afternoon, Adrianna raced from the cabin and kissed him. "I have something to tell you about Ezekiel. I think he's decided to be my protector. He watched me the entire time I was working the soil. Part of the time, he was walking not far behind me and talking. I have no idea what he was saying, but he definitely tried to talk to me. It's like having a pet."

"I'm glad Ezekiel's watching out for you. In the spring, I'll build a fence around your garden. It'll keep out deer, but you'll still need to be watchful for small predators. This Thursday I have some appointments in Deadwood. If the meetings run late, I'll have to stay overnight. Now that White Wolf's nephew is back in day school, I hope he'll stop by once in a while. If I'm not here, welcome him like this. Extend your arms, palms upward, in a welcoming gesture, and introduce yourself. If you can convince him to stay overnight, he'll sleep outside on the buffalo hide."

On Thursday evening, after giving up on Martin returning from Deadwood, Adrianna reheated a simple stew. While she was washing the dishes, she looked out the kitchen window and noticed a Lakota tying up his horse at the hitching post. From Martin's description, she was sure it was White Wolf. She dried her hands and went outside to meet him.

When she opened the door, she greeted him as Martin had said, then pointed to herself. "Adrianna. Welcome, White Wolf. I will bring you food."

She wasn't sure he'd understood, so she left the door open and went to reheat some stew. When she returned with a bowl of stew and half a loaf of bread, White Wolf's eyes lit up. She set the food on the porch and went back inside to get the buffalo hide.

Just after dark, a stunning full moon rose above the pine trees. Adrianna and White Wolf sat in silence, bearing witness to this gift. Before going back inside, Adrianna stopped at the doorway and said, "Good night, White Wolf. It was a pleasure to meet you."

He nodded to her.

The next morning, she found a bouquet of wildflowers on top of the buffalo hide. She was touched White Wolf had found such a beautiful way to thank her.

Late the next day, Martin returned home from Deadwood. Blaze neighed when Martin released him into the paddock, and Adrianna ran out to meet them. "Martin, White Wolf came here late yesterday and slept on the porch. I'm so glad I finally got to meet him. I reheated some stew for him, and he was most appreciative. Did you see the full moon last night?"

"No, the meeting ran long. I went straight to bed after a late supper and got up early for more meetings today. If we aren't too tired, maybe we could watch the moonrise tonight."

"I would like that. Also, I want to tell you one more thing. When I walked outside this morning, White Wolf had left a bouquet of wildflowers on the buffalo hide. It was such a beautiful way for him to show his appreciation."

Martin smiled. "I'm glad you two finally met. Clearly he was pleased to meet you. I hope he'll come back soon."

"Me too. We barely talked."

"This is going to sound odd, but I'm wondering if he sensed I wasn't home and came here to protect you. He perceives things on a different level. I think I told you about the time Blaze and I were caught in a blizzard near Sanborn's ranch. I'd lost my sense of direction and wasn't sure which way to go, but then Blaze whinnied. A dark, obscure shape appeared ahead of us, sometimes disappearing in the blizzard but always reappearing. It led us to Sanborn's cabin. The next time I saw White Wolf, I asked him if his spirit could have done this. He nodded and said, 'One's spirit can do many things.'

"He's the best tracker I've ever seen. He's vigilant about looking for signs like broken branches and can read tracks that are barely visible. He never uses a compass and never gets lost. He's always alert and sees and hears things before I do. I'm sorry I missed seeing him."

In May, Adrianna was planting seedlings in her garden when she noticed a black snake near the garden fence. It triggered a memory of her mother setting out a saucer of milk each day for a black snake that lived beneath their front porch. It protected her mother's garden from predators and kept other snakes away.

Adrianna ran into the cabin and returned, carefully balancing a saucer of milk. She placed it on the ground near the bottom step of the front porch. When Martin came home, she ran down the steps. "Martin, I saw a black snake near the garden this morning and set out a saucer of milk for it. My mother did this and it protected her garden from predators. I'm going to do this every day. I hope the snake will decide to live near the garden."

"Well, I hope your experiment works. I've seen evidence of rats near the stable."

In early July, White Wolf appeared just as Adrianna had finished making a blueberry pie. When she served it after supper, it was obvious he enjoyed it, so she cut another piece for him. Before he left the next morning, she brought a big piece out to the front porch for his breakfast. He smiled and nodded.

After White Wolf left, Martin took Adrianna in his arms and pulled her close. "I've never seen him look so happy."

"I need to make more pies for him."

A month later, Martin decided to walk to the law office. It was a beautiful day to leave Blaze in the pasture and take a long walk. When he returned home late that afternoon, he was pleased to see White Wolf's horse tethered in a shady spot not far from the house. Then he noticed White Wolf standing on the porch, staring through the kitchen window. White Wolf turned to look at Martin and waved.

Martin came up beside him. "Welcome, White Wolf."

White Wolf pointed to the kitchen window, which was partially open. He looked happy. "Pie."

Martin peered through the window. "Adrianna, are you making a pie?"

"Yes. I'm making a pie for White Wolf. He collected a beautiful assortment of berries and has been watching me make it. I hope he'll stay here tonight. I put the buffalo hide on the porch for him."

Martin pointed to the buffalo hide. "You will stay tonight?"

White Wolf nodded.

Adrianna spread an old tablecloth on the porch and served fried chicken, biscuits, and vegetables from her garden. Just before supper, she took the pie out of the oven to cool. Martin had never seen White Wolf look so happy.

After supper, Adrianna brought out the pie and some small plates. When she handed a piece of pie to White Wolf, he nodded to her and smiled. Later, White Wolf walked his horse to the meadow where Martin kept Blaze. Then he clambered up on a big boulder and watched the horses drink from the stream and feed on the grasses.

"Martin, I was so touched by his collecting berries for us," Adrianna said. "I came out on the porch as soon as I saw him. When he presented me with the basketful of blueberries, he smiled and said, 'Pie.' Ezekiel was quite excited about it too. White Wolf had left some berries at the base of the tree for him.

"I thanked him and said of course I'd make a pie. He stood on the porch and watched me through the kitchen window. He studied how I made the dough and rolled it out. Then, after I spread the berries over the crust and added some sugar and cinnamon, he said something. I wasn't sure what he was saying, but he pointed to the spice containers. He wanted to learn the names. So now he knows cinnamon and nutmeg. I'll be sure to send some home with him."

"I'm sure he's never forgotten the apple pie you made last fall. Do you remember how many pieces he ate? Two that night, two in the morning before he left."

Just after sunset, they walked to the pasture behind the house. There was a crescent moon and stars spilled across the sky. Martin opened a ledger that he used for legal work when he was home. Taking a pencil, he marked the stars of the Big Dipper and showed the design to White Wolf. "Big Dipper."

White Wolf studied the page and smiled. "*Wicakiyuhapi.*"

Martin marked the constellation Orion on the ledger and showed it to White Wolf.

"*Watanka.*" White Wolf nodded.

"Buffalo!" Martin was surprised. He handed the ledger and the pencil to White Wolf.

White Wolf pointed to the stars making up Orion's Belt, marked them on the ledger, and then touched his horse along the spine. Holding the ledger, he pointed to the great rectangle of Orion, marked it, and then touched both sides of his horse's ribs. Next, he marked the Pleiades star cluster, placing it outside the great rectangle, and pointed to his horse's head. Drawing on the ledger again, he marked a large spot outside the rectangle on the opposite side of Pleiades. He stood up and pointed to his horse's tail. "*Watanka.*"

Martin was fascinated. He connected the dots White Wolf had placed around his Orion sketch. He could imagine it being a buffalo. "*Watanka.*"

White Wolf smiled. Martin seldom saw him smile these days. With living conditions becoming more difficult for the Lakota, his eyes usually carried a hint of sadness. The memory of this evening would be forever etched in Martin's heart.

When they returned to the cabin, Martin spread the buffalo hide on the porch and nodded good night to White Wolf. Just as Martin and Adrianna entered their bedroom, moonlight spilled across the floor. The entire evening seemed almost ethereal to Martin. Later, after they made love, Martin held Adrianna for a long time and prayed they'd be granted a long life together.

When Martin stopped by the McGranes' to pick up Adrianna, he thought she looked a bit tired. "Did your sewing go well today?"

"Yes, but for some reason, I feel tired. It's so nice to have Rebekah's company when we both have sewing projects."

After they got home, Martin released Blaze near the barn. When he walked into the cabin, he took one look at Adrianna and said, "Are you all right?"

"Martin, I just asked your mother's pendant if I'm with child. It swung in the direction I chose for yes. I think I should meet with Mrs. Countryman, the midwife, to see what she thinks."

"Adrianna, that would be wonderful." He gently pulled her close. "I guess I shouldn't be surprised, but it takes my breath away."

In February 1882, Adrianna gave birth to their daughter, Nellie. Months ago, they'd decided, if they had a daughter, to name her after Martin's mother. After Mrs. Countryman and her assistant left, Martin looked at Adrianna holding their daughter.

"I'm so thankful you're both healthy. Later today I'll stop by the McGranes' to tell them about Nellie's birth. As we discussed, I'll ask them to be her godparents. I've never felt this kind of emotion before. I need to settle down a bit."

As soon as it was warm enough, Adrianna started working in her garden, keeping Nellie's baby basket close by so she could talk and sing to her. Martin decided to come home early one day and was surprised to see how closely Nellie was being supervised. Ezekiel kept within a yard or two of her. Whenever Adrianna moved the basket, he followed accordingly, always keeping the same distance. Even the black snake appeared more vigilant in watching out for rodents. With all this support, he trusted Nellie was going to be just fine.

In mid-July, White Wolf stopped by and brought some fish he'd caught that afternoon.

Adrianna rushed out the door the moment she saw him. "White Wolf, it's good to see you. Are these fish for our supper? Will you stay tonight?"

He nodded and handed her the fish.

"Martin's in the barn. I'll bring Nellie to you as soon as she wakes up."

He smiled and nodded again.

After supper, Martin placed Nellie's baby basket next to White Wolf. Nellie was cooing and drooling while she studied White Wolf. Then, when White Wolf softly sang her a Lakota song, she gave him a big smile. Martin's heart skipped a beat. Shortly after that, Adrianna and Nellie went to bed.

Martin looked at White Wolf. "How is your nephew who was forced to go to boarding school? Did he come home this summer?"

White Wolf nodded. "I help my sister and husband pay for train ticket. They do not have enough money. Many parents have no money to bring their children home for summer.

"I go with them to train station. After everyone leaves train, they do not see their son. There is a small child standing near the railroad tracks, but they do not know him. His head is bowed low, hair cut very short. He is very thin. When they walk to him, they find he is their son. He does not look the same. All summer he has bad dreams. He says teachers hit the students if they speak Lakota. They also force themselves on the students at night. To punish students, they make them walk for hours and sometimes beat them with carriage whips. They make children milk cows, scrub floors on hands and knees, and work in the kitchen. They make small children do school laundry. My sister and husband try to keep him home. Last week people came from boarding school and took him back. These things also happen at Christian schools."

"This is evil. It's the purposeful destruction of Lakota culture and families. If you ever need money to bring him home, you must let me know." Martin reached for his wallet. "Here is some money for your sister and husband."

Now that he and Adrianna had a child, he couldn't imagine how devastating it would be to have her taken away, sent to a school where she wasn't safe physically, mentally, or emotionally. What if a priest or teacher raped her? What if they had no money to bring her home? What if she were not allowed to return home for years?

White Horse and Martin sat on the porch and watched the moon rise. The golden moon was immense and beautiful but not beautiful enough to dispel the sadness in their hearts.

8

MARTIN WAS WORKING IN THE BARN WHEN HE OVER-heard Adrianna telling Nellie, now eighteen months old, about rainbows. "Do you see that band of colors? That's a rainbow. After it rains, always look for rainbows when the sun comes out again. Sometimes there isn't a rainbow, but the clouds can be spellbinding. Every time it rains, we'll look for a rainbow. Now let's go look at our garden."

He watched them walk hand-in-hand to the garden. Martin couldn't imagine life without them. He thought about when he fled from Chicago to Cheyenne. If not for that, he would never have met Adrianna. Was he meant to find her? How did this work? He was fascinated with the concept of destiny.

After Nellie fell asleep that evening, Martin and Adrianna sat outside on the front porch. "This afternoon I heard you tell Nellie to look for rainbows. I'm sure she will never forget that. You're such a wonderful mother. Then I gave thanks for being robbed in the Chicago stockyards. If that hadn't happened, it's quite possible I'd never have left Iowa. And, more importantly, I would never have met you."

Adrianna looked intently at Martin. "Do you believe that some things are meant to happen?"

"I wasn't raised to believe in that concept, but the longer I live, the more I wonder about it. When something occurs that seems so improbable, like my being in Deadwood the day you stepped off the stagecoach, it makes me think we were destined to meet. Perhaps there were lessons we had to learn before we could be ready for each other. We both had to leave our previous lives behind and leap into the unknown. There were no guarantees that life would be better. We only knew we had to escape from our living situations."

"So you believe it was our destiny to be together? Do you think destiny has the power to make things happen?"

Martin took Adrianna's hand and kissed it. "Well, I wouldn't phrase it quite like that, so perhaps I don't believe in destiny. Or maybe just a little bit."

Adrianna laughed and leaned into Martin.

In 1883, the U.S. Congress created and funded the Court of Indian Offenses and issued a number of bulletins that affected all natives. The *Black Hills Pioneer* printed these changes, but Martin also requested copies of the documents. He wanted to study them in detail and at his leisure. After reading them closely, he couldn't find anything beneficial for the tribes.

Ranchers had long coveted stretches of grassland on the native reservations for their cattle, and Congress had just secured this by passing legislation that broke the Great Sioux Reservation into five separate reservations. The combined land of these reservations totaled much less than the original acreage of the Great Sioux Reservation. The Lakota no longer had enough range land to generate income from their livestock. Whatever stock they had was required to feed their families. The government was now forced to buy cattle to feed the tribes.

Martin concluded that Congress instituted the Court of Indian Offenses as a ruse to strip not only land but also culture and livelihood from the natives. It outlawed most Indian ceremonies. Lakota burial and marriage practices and the use of intoxicating substances were declared criminal acts. Shaman healing ceremonies and sun dance rites were made illegal.

The *Black Hills Pioneer* had just published an article about the legislation. "*Henry Teller, Secretary of the Interior Department, stated that the real aim of this bill is to get at Indian lands and open them up to settlement. The provisions for the apparent benefit of the Indian are but a pretext to get at his lands and occupy them. If this were done in the name of greed, it would be bad enough; but to do it in the name of humanity, and under the cloak of an ardent desire to promote the Indian's welfare by making him like ourselves whether he wills it or not, is infinitely worse.*"

Martin agreed with everything Teller said. Conditions for all the tribes were only going to get worse—much worse.

In mid-May 1885, after putting Nellie to bed, Adrianna joined Martin on the front porch. "I have something to tell you."

He put his arm around her. "And just what might that be?"

"We're going to have another child. I made an appointment to meet with the midwife who delivered Nellie. I want to make sure everything is all right."

"That makes me very happy." Martin put his arm around her shoulders, and Adrianna leaned into him.

"Me too. But it's too early to say anything to Nellie."

"Yes, it is. We'll ask Rebekah to guide us with that."

In mid-November, Martin noticed that Adrianna seemed preoccupied. "Adrianna, are you feeling all right?"

"I don't feel the baby moving as much. I think we should meet with the midwife."

"I'll take you to Mrs. Countryman's later this morning. I'm sure Rebekah would be glad to have Nellie's company for a while, and Nellie will feel the same."

After Adrianna explained her concerns, Mrs. Countryman carefully felt her abdomen. "This baby is bigger than Nellie was at this point. It doesn't have much room to move. I'm sure you're very uncomfortable. Perhaps the baby will decide to come a bit early. You're close to full-term, and you're beginning to dilate."

Several days later, Martin came home around midday to check on Adrianna.

"Martin, I think my labor has started."

"I'll take Nellie to Rebekah and then ask Mrs. Countryman to come here immediately after that."

When he left Nellie with Rebekah, it was the first time she'd ever seemed reluctant to be left there, asking, "How long will I be here?"

"I don't know how long it will take for the baby to be born. I'll come back for you as soon as I can." He was trying to reassure not only Nellie but also himself, and it wasn't working very well. Adrianna was in much greater pain with this delivery.

Aware of Adrianna's approximate due date, when Mrs. Countryman opened the door, she read Martin's face in an instant. "I'll be back in a minute. I need to gather a few things. You can tell me about Adrianna's condition on the way to your home."

After seating Mrs. Countryman in his wagon, Martin headed home as fast as he dared. Sensing it was urgent, Blaze ran just fast enough to prevent the wagon from lurching side-to-side on the dirt road. Mrs. Countryman rushed from the wagon the instant Martin stopped. He left Blaze at the front porch, just in case Mrs. Countryman needed someone to assist her.

When she entered their bedroom and saw Adrianna, a cloud passed over her face. "Martin, please bring my assistant here. She lives next to Rebekah. She's excellent and should be available. Tell her I need her assistance now. The baby's in breech position."

Anxiety gripped Martin. He took a deep breath to slow his heart rate. It usually worked, but not today. He ran outside to Blaze, and they raced to get Mrs. Countryman's assistant. When she came to the door, he told her everything.

"Martin, I'll ride my horse there. I'll be there as quickly as possible."

After settling Blaze in the stable, Martin rushed to the cabin to see how Adrianna was faring. His heart stopped for a moment when he saw her. He studied her face. She was in pain and having trouble breathing. Moans came from deep inside her. He felt terrible that his love for her had created this situation.

Martin paced in and out of their bedroom. He tried to deny it, but the part of him that could foretell things knew the baby wasn't going to survive. As for Adrianna, he tried to deny she was in imminent danger, but his heart and mind knew otherwise. He took deep breaths, trying to calm his heart, trying to keep Adrianna safe through sheer force of will and love. He'd never dreamed she would have such a difficult delivery. When Nellie was born, everything had gone as well as one could possibly hope for.

He lost track of time but, at some point, the bleeding from the birth canal increased. Martin knew that meant not only the baby was injured, but Adrianna was as well. Just past midnight, Mrs. Countryman finally managed to extract the baby. The child, a little girl, was dead. Then Adrianna started hemorrhaging. She was barely conscious, her face contorted with pain.

"Martin, go to Reverend McGranes' and ask him to come here. Adrianna has lost quite a bit of blood, and her heart rate keeps fluctuating. We're trying to stabilize her. It's very serious. We're doing everything we possibly can to save her."

When Martin ran to the stable, he noticed Ezekiel sitting on the fence, keeping watch. He threw a halter on Blaze and didn't bother saddling him. It was just past midnight. The night was frigid, below freezing. Martin was shivering, but not only because of the deep cold.

Within moments of Martin knocking on the front door, Rebekah opened it.

"Mrs. Countryman asked me to have Reverend David come to our home."

"Say no more, Martin. I'll get him. And please, from now on, call him David. Don't worry about Nellie. I'm staying with her in our first-floor bedroom." She climbed the stairs quickly and quietly.

Reverend David came downstairs within minutes. "I'll be there as soon as I can. I just need to saddle my horse."

"Thank you. I'll see you at the house."

Blaze started running for home the instant he felt Martin on his back. He clearly sensed something was gravely wrong with Adrianna and that Martin was desperate. After leaving Blaze in the stable, Martin ran to the house. He took one look at Mrs. Countryman and her assistant and knew the situation had worsened. "Reverend McGrane will be here shortly."

He knelt beside the bed, took Adrianna's hand in his, and gently kissed it. Her pulse was weak. He was hoping for some kind of response, maybe some pressure from her hand on his, anything that would indicate she was conscious, but he detected nothing.

An image he'd never forgotten came to him. It was his last year in Wyoming. A freak blizzard had blown in from the northwest. He'd never seen one come in that quickly. All of the cowboys had made it back to the bunkhouse except for Joe, the youngest one. He'd only been working on the ranch for six months. Martin had taken him under his wing, like a kid brother. Trying to remember where he'd last seen him, Martin pulled on the warmest layers he possessed. "I'm going to look for Joe. He has to be somewhere close to the corral. I think I saw him heading in that direction."

The wind was howling like a wild beast, the visibility

almost zero. Martin could only see a few feet in front of him and kept within reach of the corral fence. When he reached the gate that opened onto the range, there were three head of cattle. He opened the gate to drive them into the stock-yard and then noticed a small mound near a snowdrift. After making sure the cattle were heading toward the barn, he bent down and swept snow away from the rounded shape. It was Joe. Martin slung him across his back and carried him to the bunkhouse. When he staggered inside, the cowhands carried Joe to the fireplace and swaddled him in blankets. They tried to give him hot tea with a little brandy, but it was too late. Joe never regained consciousness.

Martin feared the same with Adrianna. She wasn't responding. He looked at Reverend David kneeling on the other side of the bed, his hand lightly resting on Adrianna's shoulder, his head bowed in prayer. A shudder passed through Adrianna—her last breath. David gave her a final blessing. Martin's attempt to stifle his sobs was futile.

Mrs. Countryman pressed her lips together, trying to prevent tears from slipping down her face. "I'll stop by the under-taker's first thing tomorrow morning and ask him to come here. I deeply regret I couldn't save Adrianna and your infant daughter." Before she and her assistant left, they gathered the bloody bedding and placed a clean sheet under Adrianna. After cleaning the baby, they wrapped her in a small blanket and placed her beside Adrianna, trying to hide any disfigure-ment.

"Mrs. Countryman, would you please stop by the house and tell Rebekah about Adrianna and the baby? I'm going to stay here a bit longer with Martin." David guided Martin out of the bedroom to the kitchen table. "I want to sit with you for a while. I don't want you to be alone at this moment."

After David left, Martin spent a horrible night, mostly awake, feeling overwhelmed, his heart torn apart. And what about Nellie? He had to think clearly. His grief had to come second to caring for her. At two o'clock in the morning, he sat at the kitchen table and made a list of everything that needed to be done. It was hard to believe Adrianna was gone. He would never forget the excruciating pain she'd endured, and he felt responsible for it.

Several hours later, after getting some sleep, Martin grabbed his heavy coat and went to let Blaze outside. When he opened the stable door, Blaze was standing directly in front of him. He stepped forward, arched his head above Martin, and then lowered it, pulling Martin against him. Martin threw his arms around Blaze's neck. He understood that Blaze was trying to comfort him. "Adrianna was only with us for five years. It wasn't enough."

He decided to ride Blaze to a clearing in the forest, his private place. He often walked there to think through legal complications. Somehow, the isolation stimulated his mind to come up with workable solutions. But tonight, he went there to shout his rage at the heavens. "What kind of god are you? Do you even exist? Adrianna did nothing to deserve this."

He continued shouting until he felt weak. He sat down on a log and went quiet. His love for Adrianna had caused her death. He'd have to live with that for the rest of his life. Then he thought he heard a voice say, "You must watch over Nellie." Where did this come from? Who said that?

Martin picked himself up and headed back to the stable. He knew their little Nellie had to come first. He promised to keep his grief hidden in a corner of his heart.

When he and Blaze returned to the stable, Martin heard a swooshing noise. Ezekiel had just alit on the stall gate. He looked piercingly at Martin, then dropped his head.

Martin blinked away tears. "Ezekiel, I see your sadness. Nellie and I will feed you just like Adrianna did. Don't leave us. You brought her so much joy, dropping off gifts like the odd buttons and pieces of quartz you'd find in your explorations. Adrianna has a box of the little treasures you brought her. I hope you'll continue this tradition with Nellie. Let Nellie know you care about her too. We must all help each other."

Blaze nickered, and Martin stroked his neck. "I'm going inside. I must get some rest. We'll go to the McGranes' just after sunrise."

It just didn't seem possible that Adrianna wouldn't be there in the morning with a little sister for Nellie. And what about the funeral? He and David had discussed this before he left, but Martin couldn't remember what they agreed upon. The thought of burying Adrianna tore at his heart.

He rested for a while near the wood-burning stove, then got up and wrote a notice to post on his office door. *"My wife Adrianna and our newborn daughter passed away late last night. When the funeral arrangements have been made, I will post another notice. I plan to return to the office next week."* Martin did this with the hope of short-circuiting repeated questions about what had happened. Spearfish was a small town. He couldn't bear the thought of repeatedly responding to questions about Adrianna and the baby's passing.

After daybreak, Martin rode into town to post the notice. As they were leaving, something made Martin look back at the rooftop of the stable. Ezekiel was perched at the peak, one of his favorite resting places. He nodded to Martin and kept his eyes trained on him. Martin recognized the look of sorrow in Ezekiel's eyes. Usually, by this time of day, he was trying to rouse the household.

The town was quiet. When he rode past the McGranes' house, it was still in total darkness. He left a note at their front door saying he'd return at eight o'clock to bring Nellie home. After that, he spent some time in his office but couldn't concentrate on anything. Grief was ripping his heart apart.

When he returned to the McGranes', David opened the door. "Please come in and have a cup of coffee with us. Nellie is still asleep. If it's all right with you, Rebekah and I would like to be with you when Nellie learns about Adrianna and the baby's passing. That is, unless you feel differently."

"Thank you. I'd greatly appreciate it. I've been trying to think what I should say, and my mind just goes blank."

Rebekah embraced Martin when he came into the kitchen. "I want to help you with Nellie. There will be times when you'll feel overwhelmed with pain. Please bring her here when that happens. Also, I'd be glad to watch her when you're at work. It may seem like a long time before she'll be going to school, but that time will be here before you know it. David and I want to help you in any way we can."

"Thank you. Knowing Nellie can be with you when I'm in the office lifts a burden from me. My heart aches, and I know Nellie's will too. I promise I won't neglect her. It's just that, at this moment, it's difficult to feel anything except immense sadness and loss."

"When David was offered the position to start a church here, we decided to take it. At the time we had no idea where our children would decide to live. They now live in Illinois, in a small town on the Mississippi River, so we don't see them often. Having Nellie spend time with us will bring us joy. I've kept the books we read to our children when they were young. Nellie loves being read to and is starting to recognize some words. She will be an early reader. Don't concern yourself about asking me to watch her. She's a lovely child and is easy to have around."

David placed a hand on Martin's shoulder. "I know you feel devastated, but I also know you have an inner strength that many people don't have. It will take time, but you will come through this, and Nellie will always remember that. You two are very much alike. Also, I think the funeral should be arranged as soon as possible. There's talk of a snowstorm blowing in. Would you like me to make the arrangements?"

Martin nodded. "Whatever you suggest is fine."

The funeral service and burial took place the next morning, and snow started falling soon afterward. Late that afternoon, Martin happened to look out the kitchen window and thought he saw someone riding toward their cabin. Snowflakes blurred the image, but he realized it was White Wolf. It was unusual for White Wolf to visit them once the bitter cold set in. Martin waved to him. White Wolf signaled he'd take his horse to the stable.

"Nellie, White Wolf is here."

She jumped up and ran to the window to watch for him.

Martin opened the door, fighting back tears. "Welcome."

White Wolf nodded and stomped on the porch to remove snow from his boots.

"Do you know about Adrianna and our baby girl?"

White Wolf nodded. As soon as he set foot inside, Nellie ran to him and hugged him around his legs. White Wolf picked her up, wrapped his arms around her, and patted her back. She was sobbing so hard she started coughing. White Wolf carried her to the rocking chair. Holding her in his lap, he rocked back and forth slowly, softly chanting to her. After a while, she stopped sobbing, leaned her head against White Wolf's heart, and fell asleep.

Martin set a cup of hot tea on the table beside the rocking chair. "Thank you, White Wolf. She trusts you. She loves you. She considers you her grandfather, and so do I."

White Wolf nodded his head in acknowledgment.

There was no lack of food in the cabin. Friends and acquaintances were taking turns bringing meals to them, which was a great relief to Martin. He heated some soup for their supper and sliced a loaf of wheat bread. After supper, Nellie again fell asleep in White Wolf's lap.

Martin spread the buffalo hide out near the wood stove. "White Wolf, this is for you to sleep on." Then Martin gently lifted Nellie into his arms. "I'll take her to bed now. I've put blankets on the floor so I can be near her."

White Wolf nodded.

Martin fell asleep to the sound of White Wolf softly chanting. It was comforting. He slept, breathing with the rhythm of the chant. When he woke up in the middle of the night, everything was quiet and dark.

He sensed the presence of his mother's spirit. "I haven't felt your presence for quite some time. My heart is broken by the death of Adrianna and our infant daughter. I wish you could be here to console Nellie and me. The color of Nellie's hair is the same as yours. She's like you in so many ways and will be a wonderful woman when she grows up. I miss your presence in my life."

He rolled onto his side, trying to find a comfortable position to fall asleep. At that moment, he felt a soft touch across his forehead, so light it felt like a breath of air or the delicate brush of a feather. He closed his eyes. Before he drifted off to sleep, the following thought came to him: *Write down and remember what life has given you. When you're traveling down a dark road, in spite of your losses, remember to count your blessings.*

When Martin went to stoke the fire in the morning, White Wolf was gone but the gift of his presence lingered. Martin forced himself to eat. He was determined to keep himself strong and present for Nellie and not let grief be his sole companion. He also had several cases that required immediate attention. Somehow life would go on.

Time passed in a blur for Martin, with the hours passing into days, and days into weeks. He kept following one thought with another, completing one action after another. He was functioning but still felt so very empty inside. He never neglected Nellie, but the pain of loss often hovered over his shoulder, fighting for part of his heart. Whenever she woke up in the middle of the night crying, Martin hauled the buffalo hide into her room and slept there. After he returned to working regular hours at the law office, Rebekah insisted on having Nellie stay with her. She told him his heart would heal one day, but right now he couldn't imagine it.

The week before Christmas, Martin dressed Nellie in her warmest clothes, gathered her in his arms, and hitched Blaze to their small wagon.

"Papa, where are we going?"

"We're going to the edge of the forest so you can pick out a Christmas tree for our cabin. After we chop it down, I'll help you decorate it."

She smiled when he put his arm around her. "Do you remember where Mama's little ornaments are?"

Martin nodded his head. "Of course. It'll be a wonderful little Christmas tree."

Adrianna had created beautiful ornaments from scraps of fabric. She'd even made pinecones look festive by tying tiny ribbons on them. He tried to repeat what she'd done so Nellie could have some sense of wonder about Christmas.

"On Christmas day, we'll have dinner with the McGranes. I have some little gifts for them that I'd like you to help me wrap."

Christmas Eve in Martin's family had always been a modest affair. His father always took the boys to chop down a small pine tree from the windbreak on their farm. Then, after he and his brothers dragged it back to the house, they decorated the tree with strings of popcorn and cranberries. The decorations were simple, but it was all they knew, and it made them happy.

Before going to bed, Martin set out several gifts under their little tree. Rebekah had knitted a sweater and slippers for Nellie, and he'd bought a small stuffed bear and new coat for her. When Nellie opened her gifts the next morning, she seemed pleased but part of her looked lost. How could she not? Martin was sure his features carried the same expression.

Later that morning, he and Nellie attended Reverend David's Christmas service. When Rebekah sat down next to them, Nellie climbed onto her lap and stayed there the entire service. Afterward, they went to the McGranes' for Christmas dinner. Rebekah and David had some little gifts for Nellie to open, and they gave Martin a couple of books for him to read to Nellie at bedtime.

Several days later, David stopped by Martin's law office. "Good morning, Martin. I wanted to check on you and see if there's anything I could do."

"Thanks to you and Rebekah, we're managing all right. It's an incredible gift for both of us that Nellie can spend her days with Rebekah. I should be paying her to do this."

"You know she wouldn't hear of it. She isn't caring for Nellie because she misses our grandchildren. She genuinely loves her. One more thing. I think you're showing incredible strength with how you're managing the loss of Adrianna and your infant daughter. Some people become bitter."

"I'm not bitter. I'm just lost."

Martin usually looked forward to the start of a new year. He always tied up any loose ends with clients and made sure they were ready for the coming year. Also, Adam Cranston was spending less time in the office and gradually referring some clients to Martin. Normally Martin would have taken this in stride, even enjoyed it, but he felt depleted. No one had said anything, but he knew he was having difficulty anticipating his clients' needs. And where had his intuitions gone? He'd always taken these abilities for granted.

In mid-January, he decided to have a chat with Reverend David at his office. If he timed it right, Nellie would still be napping. When he rapped on the door, David looked surprised to see him so early.

"Martin, you're here early. Is everything all right?"

"Not exactly. I was hoping you might be able to give me some advice. I'm having difficulty anticipating my clients' needs. Until now, that was never a problem for me. I've always had intuitions about my cases and what I needed to do for my clients. I don't want to lose any clients. I expect it's because I'm still so wounded from the loss of Adrianna and the baby."

"First of all, your clients—and I know a fair number of them—hold you in high esteem. They have great sympathy for you and what you're going through. And here's another thing. A week ago, you didn't even recognize this loss of perception. The fact that you're now aware of it means your ability to read situations is beginning to return.

"It's your heart that will require time to heal. The only way around that kind of pain is through it. You're a strong man, physically and emotionally. I have no doubt about your ability to heal from your tragic loss. You two were very devoted to each other. You will always carry her in your heart."

In mid-March, Martin left Nellie with Rebekah and went to Adrianna's grave. The snowpack had finally melted. He could see her gravesite and touch the earth that covered her. The wellspring of tears since her passing had mostly run dry, but the pain in his heart was still intense. No one else was at the cemetery, so he spoke aloud to her.

"My beloved Adrianna, we're very fortunate to have Rebekah and David assuming the role of grandparents for our Nellie. She loves being read to and is reading a little bit on her own. I'm not much of a cook, so we usually have supper at one of the cafés. I read to her before she goes to bed, and we always say a prayer for you and the baby. I promise I will always protect her. My darling, I miss you so very much."

When Martin headed back to town, he felt a sense of hope for the first time in months. The wind held just a hint of spring, a glimmer of something better. Also, his legal skills were finally back on track, which was a great relief to him.

The brightest spot in his days was stopping at the McGranes' to pick up Nellie. She always ran to him so he could swoop her into his arms. Then Blaze would nicker, asking Nellie to stroke his neck before getting into the wagon. Sometimes they had an early supper at the café and oftentimes Rebekah sent food home with them. Somehow time was passing, and the ache in his heart was less intense.

9

A FEW DAYS LATER, MARTIN AND NELLIE WERE WALKING on a path behind their cabin when they heard a faint whimpering cry. Martin picked up Nellie and turned off the path to follow the sound. After walking about twenty yards, Martin stepped behind a large pine tree and found a wolf cub. It was nestled against its mother, who had been shot and killed.

"Papa, set me down." Nellie ran to the whimpering cub, bent down, and started petting it. When Martin tried to pull her back, she started crying. "We have to save the little wolf. It's like me. It doesn't have a mama. It needs food. Look, it's a girl. We must save her. We must protect her."

Martin could see Adrianna's determination in Nellie. If Adrianna were there, he was sure she would also try to save the pup. "Nellie, I don't think that's a good idea. She'll be too wild for us to control."

"Papa, she will not be too wild. I'll train her. She will grow up to guard us."

"If she has tasted wild food, it'll be too late to prevent her from killing for it."

"Look at the mother. She was still feeding her cub. Papa, you have to let me bring her home. She's like me. Her mother is gone." Nellie started sobbing.

Martin tried to put an arm around her, but she pulled away.

"Lord help me," Martin said under his breath. Nellie was

sobbing, hugging the cub so tight it was squirming. He could count on one hand the number of times he'd seen her cry this hard. No matter what—bumps, bruises—she always got right back up. No tears.

"All right, Nellie. We'll take her home, but if we're not able to tame her, we'll have to release her."

"She will never leave me." Before he could say anything, Nellie picked up the cub, wrapped her arms around it, and held it across her chest. She looked fiercely at him. "I will protect her." She let the cub suck on her finger while they walked back home.

Just as they approached the stable, Martin spotted White Wolf's horse in the meadow near their cabin. He was waiting on the front porch and smiled when he saw the wolf cub in Nellie's arms. White Wolf extended his arms and opened his hands. Without saying a word, Nellie gently placed the cub in White Wolf's hands. Martin noticed she did this without any resistance, implicitly trusting White Wolf. Then they all went into the cabin.

"You have a little sister now. We must feed her. Bring milk and cloth." White Wolf sat near the fireplace and gently stroked the cub.

"Nellie, get a small cloth from your mother's sewing drawer. I'll warm some milk."

She hurried back to White Wolf and handed him the cloth. Martin fought back tears. Some kind of shift was taking place, a turning point in his and Nellie's relationship. He wasn't sure what it was, but it was significant.

"Nellie, the milk is ready. Come here and bring it to White Wolf. He'll show you how to feed the cub."

She walked slowly to White Wolf, looking so very serious, making sure not a drop of milk spilled. Martin's heart ached. He wished Adrianna's spirit could witness this. After Nellie set the bowl beside White Wolf, she handed him the cloth and sat next to him. He twisted a corner of the rag, dipped it in the milk, and placed it in the cub's mouth. After doing this several times, he placed the cub in Nellie's lap. "You feed her."

Nellie dipped the cloth just like White Wolf had shown her. When the cub no longer seemed interested in eating, Nellie hugged her gently and hummed a little song. The cub nestled against her and fell asleep. Nellie kept gently petting the cub. "She needs a name."

"Hakáta." White Wolf looked at Nellie. "It means 'little sister of a girl.'"

Nellie smiled at him. "My Hakáta."

Martin's heart gave in to what he was witnessing. There was a new addition to their family. He had to admit the wolf cub was striking. Her ebony coat was beautiful, and her eyes reflected intelligence, even at such a young age. Most important of all, this was the happiest he'd seen Nellie since Adrianna's passing.

Martin brought bread, cheese, and sausage to the table for their supper. Afterward, White Wolf spread the buffalo hide near the front door. "I stay two nights. Hakáta sleeps with me."

Martin looked at White Wolf and nodded. "Thank you. We'll watch how you handle the cub. How old is she?"

"Maybe one moon. Her eyes are blue. In one or two moons they will turn gold."

"What about her color? I've never seen a black wolf."

White Wolf looked at Martin and Nellie. "Her color is not usual. As she grows, she will reveal her purpose. She is here to protect Nellie. One day she will be your big sister."

Martin's eyes glazed with tears. The past year had left him feeling hollowed out. He was trying to be a good father to Nellie but felt he often came up short. Maybe this beautiful little creature would bring harmony and comfort into their home.

"Papa, may I sleep on the floor tonight?"

"Not tonight. We must let White Wolf comfort the cub

and train her a bit. You may spend all day with them tomorrow. Then tomorrow night you may sleep with them."

"After White Wolf leaves, I want her to sleep in my room."

"Is there anything else you've decided?"

Nellie smiled at him. "Not yet."

"She may sleep on the old horse blanket in your room. That should keep her warm. We'll see how this all works out." Without thinking about it, Martin realized he'd just accepted Nellie as Hakáta's mistress.

When spring arrived, Martin decided it was time for Hakáta to start sleeping in the stable. One night, when they were sitting on the front porch, Martin said, "Nellie, Hakáta is now old enough to sleep in the stable. You know how much she likes being outside. That will allow her to go in and out as she pleases."

"But what if she runs away?"

Martin shook his head. "She would never run away from you. She accepts you as her mistress and will always be loyal to you. Even at her young age, she's very protective of you. Wolves are meant to live outside. You might not have noticed, but once she knows you're awake, you two are inseparable."

Nellie smiled. "I know, Papa."

"Andrew Sanborn considers wolves the smartest creatures he's ever come across. If you watch Hakáta, you'll see she's always sniffing the air. She picks up scents from prey that are crossing the valley. Sometimes during the night, I hear her growling. She's warning prey to stay away. She's protecting us."

On those nights when Martin had trouble sleeping, he roamed around the cabin and checked to see if Hakáta was on the front porch. She was always there, sometimes awake. The first time he didn't see her, he was worried, concerned she'd gone off to hunt something. Then he saw her circling the house like a guard dog. He smiled and relaxed. It was reassuring to know she protected them. In fact, it was more than reassuring; he felt safer. He had an assistant.

In May, Martin rode Blaze to Adrianna's grave. "I was thinking about you and decided to come here instead of having dinner in town. Nellie and I have planted some vegetables in your garden. It's been very dry. We water the garden every evening. Nellie can barely manage it, but she likes to use your watering can. We miss you so very much. I can't stay long. Adam and I have a heavy caseload, which is good."

On the ride back to the office, Martin realized he was feeling less numb inside. He was also thinking sharply again, which was a huge relief. Now that he thought about it, the same thing seemed to be happening with Nellie. After Adrianna's passing, Rebekah had said Nellie wasn't interested in being read to. Mostly she just wanted to be near Rebekah. Earlier this week, though, when he stopped to pick up Nellie, Rebekah pulled him aside. She said that Nellie had brought a book to her and asked her to read it. Both their hearts were beginning to heal.

Martin received a letter from James in September, mostly commenting about how quickly their two boys were growing up. He also mentioned the drought conditions around Cheyenne. *"This summer has been the driest and hottest that anyone can remember in eastern Wyoming. Montana is in trouble too. In many places there's no grass for the cattle to feed on. Once all this is past, we hope you and Nellie will visit us."* That evening, Martin wrote to James, confirming the same dire conditions in the Dakota Territory and promising to come to Cheyenne with Nellie someday.

In mid-September, they were sitting on the front porch when Ezekiel started squawking. Hakáta jumped off the porch and ran to the edge of their property, sniffing the air.

"I think White Wolf is coming to visit us. I don't understand how Ezekiel knows these things."

"I hope he's right, Papa. I've missed him."

Within minutes they saw White Wolf heading toward them. When he came riding into their yard, Nellie ran to him, shouting his name.

Martin followed her. "Welcome, White Wolf. Will you stay with us tonight?"

White Wolf nodded.

Martin went inside and returned with the blankets he reserved for White Wolf. Whenever White Wolf stayed on the front porch, Hakáta always slept near him. He had never liked the confinement of the cabin, and Hakáta felt the same. She only slept inside when it was dangerously cold.

White Wolf always kept his rifle near him through the night. Even when sleeping, he was alert and would hear things before Martin did. Martin would never forget the only time he'd asked White Wolf if he wanted to sleep in their cabin. His response was, "I cannot sleep inside a cabin. It is like a trap. A teepee breathes."

"Could you play a bead game with Nellie while I get supper ready?"

Another nod and a smile.

While Martin was fixing supper, he watched them from the kitchen window. Suddenly Nellie set down her beads and looked at White Wolf. "Will you be my grandpa?"

White Wolf nodded his head. "You call me 'Tukàšila.' Lakota for 'grandfather.' It is our secret with your papa."

"What about Hakáta? Will you be her grandpa too?"

White Wolf nodded and smiled. "She knows this."

Nellie leaned against him and knitted her arm through his.

After supper, White Wolf and Nellie played games until she curled up on her blanket and fell asleep. Martin tucked the blanket around her. "I've been waiting for her to fall asleep. I have some questions for you. I've seen many game birds flying south—pheasants, grouse, geese, ducks. This is early. Have you seen this before?"

White Wolf shook his head. "Also quail and doves. When the days grow short, they know it is time to leave. But this year they leave early. They know something. Spring gave us little rain. The hot summer sun burned dry prairie grass to the roots and dried up our water. Small creeks have little or no water. The rivers run low. There is not enough for birds to eat. There are many fires on the range. Winter will be hard on man and all animals."

"Blaze's coat is the thickest I've ever seen it at this time of year. Ranchers tell me the coats on their cattle are very thick. It's also happening in Montana and Wyoming. I received a letter from my friend in Cheyenne. He said this summer was the driest that anyone could remember in eastern Wyoming. In many places there's no grass for the cattle to feed on."

White Wolf nodded. "In August I see beavers make big wood piles. You must also gather wood. Pile it around your house. The animals see hard winter coming. We must get ready too. I leave early in the morning. I will not see you for long time. I will shelter with my family."

Early the next morning, Martin brought coffee and biscuits to the front porch. Nellie was already sitting beside White Wolf, excited about eating breakfast on the porch. There was not much talking. Martin studied White Wolf's face. He looked unusually serious, preoccupied.

"White Wolf, I have something to give you before you leave. I'll get it now."

Martin walked to the stable and pulled down the buffalo hide from the shelf where he stored it during the warm months. He returned to the front porch and laid it at White Wolf's feet. "During the night I woke up and remembered what you said about the coming winter. I'm sure you are right. The buffalo hide will help keep you warm this winter."

White Wolf looked into Martin's eyes and nodded.

Martin blinked back tears, recognizing this was a pivotal point in their friendship. Part of him knew they might never see White Wolf again. So much had been stripped from all the tribes over the past decades. Most of the best land had been taken by the government with their various schemes or sold to settlers when the tribes desperately needed money. Natives no longer had enough arable land to survive on, and it wasn't just land that was being taken. Many of their children were being forced to attend distant schools where they were treated brutally. Some never returned home.

Martin and Nellie stood on the porch and watched White Wolf ride off. Just before he disappeared from view, he stopped his horse and turned to wave. Martin and Nellie waved back. Martin tried to hide his concern from Nellie. It was going to be a brutal winter. He hoped White Wolf would survive.

"Papa, White Wolf said he will not see us for a long time. How long will it be? It makes me sad to see him ride away. He looks sad too."

"My darling Nellie, I'm sad too. All the animals are giving us signs that it will be a hard winter."

"Yesterday I asked White Wolf to be my grandpa and also Hakáta's. He said yes."

"I'm sure that made him happy. He cares very much about you, but we should only tell our best friends."

"Why?"

"Because there are narrow-minded people who wouldn't understand. White Wolf is trying to protect you from those people. They can be mean."

"Papa, are we wide-minded people?"

"Yes, people like White Wolf, Mrs. Rebekah, Reverend David, our close friends, and you and I are broad-minded people. That means we try not to judge someone just because they're different from us. There's an expression—don't judge someone until you have walked in their shoes. That's what I try to do."

The next day, after leaving Nellie with Rebekah, Martin rode to Deadwood to meet with Karl Johnson, the newspaper editor. There were a couple of cases Martin wanted to discuss with him. He was a good source of background information, and they each trusted the other to be discreet.

After they finished discussing the cases, Johnson asked, "What do you know about the drought?"

"There was a small prairie fire several miles from my place a week ago, and a group of us managed to put it out. My Lakota friend doesn't recall it ever being this dry. The streams are so low the Lakota are struggling to find water for themselves and grass for their horses. He said beavers are collecting the most wood he's ever seen them gather. Birds are flying south earlier than usual.

"My crow has been gone for at least a week. He's never left this early before. Temperatures have been cooler than usual. Given all that, it might be a while before I see you again. Thanks very much for your time today."

Martin was walking to the stable when he noticed the bar owner who'd wanted to hire Adrianna heading his way. He crossed to the other side of the street to avoid him, but the bar owner did the same. When Martin tried to ignore him and walk past him, the owner confronted him and taunted him about Adrianna's passing. Usually self-restrained, Martin slammed his fist into the man's jaw, knocking him down onto the wooden sidewalk. The bar owner was stunned and couldn't stand up. Roiling inside, Martin didn't look back and kept walking to the stable.

October was dry and not unusually cool but, after considering White Wolf's comments, Martin started chopping wood and stacked it around the barn and the base of the house. On weekends, he hitched Blaze to their flatbed wagon so he and Nellie could search for fallen timber. She liked these excursions, always trying to spy a fallen tree or branch before Martin did. By the end of October, they'd accumulated a considerable amount of chopped wood. Martin was beginning to wonder if he was being overly cautious. He kept looking for signs of a threatening winter. Blaze and Hakáta's coats were definitely heavier than normal. What did their bodies know that he didn't?

It started snowing in early November 1886 and never stopped. Martin had never seen anything like it. Cattle were suffering badly. After a difficult summer with inadequate nourishment, the herds were in no condition to weather a harsh winter. On the first anniversary of Adrianna's passing, a blizzard raged. It was the coldest November Martin could ever remember. He moved their mattresses near the potbellied stove because the bedroom was frigid.

Martin and Nellie made a pine wreath for Adrianna's grave to observe the first year of her passing, but it was impossible to go to the cemetery. "Nellie, instead of going to your mama's grave, we'll hang the wreath on our garden fence. It's too dangerous to go to the cemetery." He dressed Nellie in her warmest clothes, wrapped a heavy blanket around her, and trudged to the garden, carrying her with the wreath slung over his arm.

"Adrianna, Nellie made this beautiful pine wreath for you. She found the little pinecones and helped tie the red ribbon. You are ever-present in our thoughts and our hearts. The love you gave to us is part of who we are. It will never leave us."

"Mama, I will always love you. I miss you." Nellie looked up at Martin. "I think she knows we're here."

"I do too. The wind is picking up. We need to go back inside."

Unless there was a snowstorm, Martin went into the office every day and picked up Nellie well before sunset. When they entered the cabin, the first thing he did was add more wood to the potbellied stove and stoke the fire. Hakáta spent the day in the stable, going in and out as she pleased, but as soon as Nellie and Martin came home, she ran to her favorite corner and lay down on her rug.

At suppertime, Nellie always climbed up onto her chair to sit on an overstuffed pillow. The next step in her routine was arranging the salt and pepper shakers on the table. She always adjusted them a bit, usually setting them close together. Her sense of order amused Martin. It was the same with her books, as well as her rock and mineral collection.

One evening, when they started to eat, the salt and pepper shakers moved the tiniest bit, leaving a separation between them.

Nellie looked at Martin with big eyes. "Papa, did you see that?"

"Yes, I did. I think your mother is letting us know she's watching over us."

Nellie smiled. "I think so too."

In the middle of the night, Adrianna appeared to Martin in a dream. "You're a good father. Hakáta will help you protect Nellie." He woke up and had trouble shaking off the dream. Could Adrianna's spirit have guided him and Nellie to the wolf cub, its mother dead, just like Adrianna? It was too much to think about. He turned over and tried to fall back asleep.

In early January 1887, a blizzard blew in with fierce winds and dropped over eighteen inches of snow across the Dakota, Wyoming, and Montana territories. Then rain fell and temperatures dropped to fifty degrees below zero. Any grass that had existed was now sealed beneath a deep layer of snow and ice.

Martin and Nellie didn't leave the cabin for almost a week. He was thankful Rebekah and David had given Nellie a little chalkboard for Christmas. They played endless games of pig-in-a-poke and tic-tac-toe on it. Martin also made up games with the alphabet and basic numbers that Rebekah had taught Nellie. It kept them both occupied until bedtime.

After a lull, another big snowstorm developed in February. Laramie, Wyoming, reported frozen snow four feet deep on the stage route, and Miles City, Montana, recorded a temperature of sixty below zero. That storm kept Martin and Nellie homebound for the better part of a week.

Two months later, the spring thaw revealed cattle carcasses littered across the plains and in stream beds. Local newspapers estimated a ninety-percent loss of cattle in the northern ranges of the Dakota, Montana, and Wyoming territories. They also reported that over 300 cowboys and settlers in remote cabins had frozen to death. The train line to Rapid City that had been established the previous year wouldn't be carrying many cattle east this year.

In late April, Martin rode to Andrew Sanborn's ranch to see how his operation had fared.

"Martin, thanks for stopping by."

"I haven't seen you in town and have been concerned about how your ranch survived the Big Die-Up. I'd also like to know what you think is going to happen with the cattle industry."

"I just made some coffee. Let's talk about it on the front porch. I sold off about half my herd last September, so I should be able to hold onto my ranch, but here's what I think is going to happen. Ranchers will have to recognize the days of the open range are over. Cattle herds will need to be smaller. Instead of depending on the range to feed their stock, ranchers will have to become farmers and grow crops to feed their herds. Also, they'll probably have to sell some of the crops for income. I know three ranchers who are walking away from it all. They don't have the money to keep operating their ranches, even at a reduced level.

"Also, barbed wire will soon be used to define a rancher's property line and prevent herds from ranging too far. I think Spearfish will continue to be a vital community for the area, but there will be fewer cowboys around. Two of my men left this spring, and I'm not replacing them. I'm sure other ranchers are making the same decision. Also, a few bars might have to shut down."

Martin smiled. "If that's the worst of it, we'll be lucky. I expect in the long run the law firm will be fine, but we'll need to tighten our belts for a while. On a different note, what do you think about the Dawes Act that the U.S. Congress passed in February?"

Sanborn grasped his coffee mug with both hands. "I've read what the local papers have reported, and here's what concerns me. Traditionally tribes have owned their land communally, not individually. This act will change that, and I don't think it bodes well for the tribes. My understanding is that land will be allotted to individual natives who meet some given definition, rather than the tribal group. These allotments will amount to significantly less land than the tribes originally possessed and will provide a land base for pioneer settlement.

"The bill was drafted and passed the U.S. Senate without consent or input from any tribal members or their leaders. It's the government's way of stripping land away from the tribes. I'm not sure the tribes understand the act but, even if they did, the U.S. government is committed to doing this.

"I believe the main purpose of the act is to reduce the amount of native-owned land and then open the remaining land to non-tribal settlement and development by the railroads."

"Andrew, I think you're right. What you just said is better than any summary I've read. Each time the government breaks a treaty, no matter how they couch it, they end up seizing more tribal land."

In mid-September, White Wolf appeared late on a Friday afternoon. Nellie was outside checking on her pumpkin patch when she spotted him. She waved to him and raced inside to tell Martin.

"Papa, White Wolf is coming to see us. Maybe we could go hunting with him tomorrow."

"I think that's a good idea. We haven't seen him in such a long time. Since you're now in first grade, you're probably old enough to ride along on the buckboard and watch us hunt."

Nellie raced to the stable and opened the paddock gate for White Wolf's horse. Now that she was in first grade, she was very determined to do more grown-up things. That evening they talked about where to hunt the next day. "I'd like to hunt near the creek where we go fishing. White Wolf, is that all right with you?"

White Wolf nodded in agreement.

"And Miss Nellie, is that all right with you?"

"Yes, Papa. I'm excited to go hunting. May Hakáta come along?"

"Of course."

When they left the cabin at daybreak, Martin hoisted Nellie onto the wagon seat, wrapped a blanket around her, then sandwiched her between him and Hakáta. Both the wolf and Nellie looked excited, as did White Wolf, riding close beside them.

After the previous harsh winter, White Wolf and Martin weren't sure what to expect in terms of prey, but they were hoping to find pheasant and deer. After they were well out of town and near the forest, Martin saw Hakáta turn her head into the wind. She had caught the scent of some kind of prey. Sometimes she brought rabbits back to their cabin but didn't kill them. She left that to Martin. He wondered what kind of scent she had picked up.

White Wolf was an excellent hunter. He also watched Hakáta closely to see where her nose was pointing. About half a mile away, a young buck ran out of the woods. White Wolf signaled with his hand to Hakáta, and she jumped down from the wagon. The two of them raced toward the deer. Martin and Nellie followed in the wagon as quickly and safely as they could. Martin didn't want a broken axle. He looked across at Nellie. She was fascinated with what was taking place.

When they reached the point where White Wolf had entered the woods, Martin stopped the wagon. He and Nellie listened for any indication of White Wolf and Hakáta's location. Suddenly the crack of White Wolf's rifle shattered the silence. After lots of thrashing, a deer leaped out of the woods. One more shot from White Wolf's rifle took the deer down.

Hakáta raced out from the pine trees and ran to the deer. She froze and looked back. Martin was watching for White Wolf to appear, but he allowed Blaze to pull the wagon in the direction of the deer. Suddenly White Wolf charged out of the woods on his horse and ran straight to the deer.

Martin and White Wolf loaded the deer into the back of the wagon and headed back to the cabin, where they strung up the deer from a tree limb. After a simple supper on the front porch, they walked into the field beyond the stable to look for constellations. Stars sparkled across the entire night sky. White Wolf and Martin pointed out constellations to Nellie, telling her the Lakota and English names for them.

10

IN LATE NOVEMBER 1887, MARTIN AND NELLIE WENT TO the cemetery to observe the second anniversary of Adrianna's passing.

"Mama, I asked Papa if I could talk first. I think of you every day, and I'm taking good care of your garden. The flowers didn't look too good this year because there wasn't much rain. My wolf Hakáta tries to watch over me, so don't worry about me. I miss you and will always love you. I carry you in my heart."

"My dearest Adrianna, as you can tell from what Nellie just said, we think of you every day and are trying to carry on the traditions you created for our family. You are still part of us. I will always carry you in my heart."

In terms of weather conditions, December passed uneventfully. Everyone was hoping there would be no repeat of the January 1887 blizzard, but that changed in the early morning hours of January 12, 1888. A howling wind and the snap of a tree branch woke Martin. He looked out the kitchen window, only to find a complete whiteout. He stirred the embers in the fireplace and added more logs to the smoldering ashes. He and Nellie would not be venturing out today.

Just before dusk, it finally stopped snowing. Before Martin went to bed, he opened the front door, only to find a five-foot snowdrift blocking his exit. He had no choice but to wait until morning and shovel snow from the back door to the stable.

When Martin returned to his office two days later, he read both the Spearfish and Deadwood newspapers. Livestock losses were severe. Thousands of cattle brought up from the south couldn't withstand the frigid weather of the northern plains. When the storm passed east of the Missouri River, it had become even more deadly. At noon, snow and ice were melting from windows, but by 3:30 p.m. temperatures had dropped well below zero. The storm came in so quickly that dozens of schoolchildren and hundreds of settlers died. Newspapers reported hurricane-force winds.

After Martin finished reading the articles, he was deeply shaken. He knew it was irrational, but the reports made him think about the possibility of losing Nellie. What if that storm had hit the Black Hills instead? He didn't know how he could go on living without her.

In April, James came to visit Martin and Nellie. Martin met him at the stagecoach stop, with Blaze pulling their small wagon. James grabbed Martin's shoulder and shook his hand. "Martin, it's so good to see you. You look just the same. Well, except for a little bit of gray in your hair."

Martin laughed. "And I could say the same for you. Nellie is very excited about your visit. You'll get to meet her after school. We'll head to my office now. I'll give you a quick tour of Spearfish on the way there."

"So you haven't retired Blaze?"

"He's semi-retired, but I knew you two would want to see each other. I'm training another horse and will soon give Blaze to Nellie. We'll have an early supper at a café and then spend the evening at home. Nellie and I want to hear all about your family. Once the railroad runs between here to Cheyenne, we'll take a trip to see your family."

"They'd like that very much. I decided to make this trip

alone because I wanted to make sure you two were all right. We were so very sorry to learn of Adrianna and the baby's passing. I can only spend two nights away from my family and business."

"I appreciate any time you can give us. It's been over two years since Adrianna and the baby passed. We have wonderful friends, the Episcopal minister and his wife, who have been supportive to us this entire time. I don't know how we could have managed without them. They've become like grandparents to Nellie, and she considers you to be her uncle."

"I'm pleased to hear that."

Martin was so engaged in talking to James that he lost track of time. Hakáta had been pacing the office and pawing Martin's legs to get his attention. Finally Martin glanced at his watch.

"James, excuse me for a moment." Martin walked to the office door and opened it. "Hakáta, get Nellie."

Martin watched the wolf fly down the wooden sidewalk and disappear around the corner, heading to the school. "Nellie has been begging me for months to let Hakáta meet her at school and walk back to the office with her. I've been hesitant to allow it. She's everything I have. I could never forgive myself if something happened to her."

Martin had been counting the minutes since Hakáta raced to get Nellie and was about to leave for the school when they flew into the office.

"Papa, thank you for sending Hakáta to get me." When she noticed James, she stopped talking.

"Nellie, this is my friend James. You've heard me talk about him many times. He came all the way from Cheyenne to see us."

"Your father was telling me about Hakáta. She's beautiful."

"Thank you. She's my little sister. She also protects me."

"Well, she looks like your big sister to me." James smiled at Nellie, and she laughed. "I have never seen a black wolf before. Did you know that one dog year is equivalent to seven years in human life? So that means if Hakáta is about eighteen months old, she is roughly ten years old in human terms, which makes her older than you. She's beautiful."

Nellie smiled and hugged Hakáta.

"Your father is like a brother to me, which makes me your Uncle James, my wife your Aunt Anna, and our two boys Samuel and Nathan your cousins. Sometimes good friends are closer than family."

That evening, James taught Nellie some card games he played with his sons. Eventually she crawled into Martin's lap and fell asleep to the cadence of old friends sharing remembrances.

Several months after James's visit, a federal commission came to Lakota territory with a proposal to break the Lakota Nation into six reservations. When Martin learned about it, he went to Deadwood to talk to A.W. Merrick, the newspaper editor.

Merrick waved Martin into his office. "It's good to see you. You always have a reason for coming here. I wonder what it is today."

"Well, I'm here because I'd like to talk about the proposed changes in the reservation boundaries. They're supposed to take effect in 1890. It looks like our national government is about to strip more land from the current reservations."

"You're right about that. A congressional delegation came here with a proposal to carve up the Lakota Nation into six small reservations. By doing that, the U.S. government will be able to open nine million acres to non-native settlement. They're offering the Lakota a dollar-fifty per acre. I don't think it's fair. The Lakota are having a difficult time surviving the way things are right now. When this goes through, the small reservation areas will be surrounded on all sides by settlers."

In late September, Martin and Nellie were raking leaves when White Wolf rode into their yard. They were thrilled to see him. Nellie ran over to pet his horse and then threw her arms around White Wolf's neck when he bent down to her.

Martin gripped White Wolf's shoulders. "Welcome. We have missed you. Can you stay with us tonight?"

White Wolf nodded and handed Martin two pheasants. "For supper."

"Thank you. We'll have it with some freshly baked bread from Mrs. Rebekah."

Martin was relieved to see White Wolf, but concern weighed on his heart. White Wolf was thinner, as was his horse, and the air of sadness he'd carried these past years was deeper. From the expression on White Wolf's face, Martin knew he was there to say goodbye. Martin looked at Nellie and Hakáta. Without anything being said, he was sure they also sensed it.

Martin took the pheasants inside and left Nellie and Hakáta with White Wolf so they could talk. He opened the kitchen window. Martin felt a bit guilty about eavesdropping, but he wanted to hear what White Wolf was saying to Nellie. He seemed to be giving her some final advice.

"When a person talks to you, do not only listen to the words—look into their eyes. Then you will know if they speak true or if they lie."

"I will do that. I will remember everything you say. I wish you could stay with us."

White Wolf smiled and patted Nellie's hand. "I must stay with my sister and her family."

When it was time to eat, Martin spread an old blanket on the porch. Hakáta sank down beside White Wolf and leaned against him.

"Thank you for coming here. Tomorrow we'll ride in the

wagon and carry this buffalo hide for you. When we're close to your home, we'll put it on a travois."

White Wolf nodded.

They sat mostly in silence, watching a crescent moon travel slowly across the indigo sky, its path lit by myriads of stars.

After breakfast, Martin packed hardtack and sausage into a flour sack for White Wolf and handed it to him when he climbed onto the buckboard. White Wolf sat next to Nellie, while his horse and Hakáta kept pace with the wagon. Years ago, Martin had hunted in the area but never gone this far.

When they approached Wounded Knee Creek, White Wolf motioned for Martin to stop. He stepped down from the buckboard, and Martin handed the buffalo hide to him. After securing the hide to a travois, White Wolf signaled for Hakáta to come to him.

Understanding that White Wolf wanted to speak to Hakáta, Martin and Nellie kept their distance. He spoke softly to her for a while, both looking very sad. Hakáta looked into his eyes and leaned against him. Martin was sure White Wolf was telling Hakáta to watch over Nellie.

When White Wolf turned to him and Nellie, Martin choked up, knowing this farewell would be a final one. "We will miss you. You will always be welcome in our home. My heart is heavy."

There were so many other things he wanted to say. *I will always remember that you saved my life. I would not have this wonderful daughter if not for you. I will always treasure your friendship. Thank you for being Nellie and Hakáta's grandfather. I'm concerned about you. I fear for your life. I hate the sickness in this country that is killing native people, taking your children from you, trying to undermine your beliefs.* He looked into White Wolf's eyes and was sure the Lakota understood what Martin was thinking.

When White Wolf turned toward Nellie, she threw her arms around his waist. "I will miss you, Tuŋkášila. I will think of you every day."

Hakáta whined and leaned against White Wolf.

White Wolf mounted his horse, then looked at them. "One day, long after my time, there will be a reckoning."

Hakáta began howling.

When he reached the crest of a hill, White Wolf stopped and turned back to them, extending his hand in farewell. Martin and Nellie did the same. Hakáta kept howling after he disappeared over the hill.

Martin turned the wagon toward home, and Hakáta settled between Nellie and Martin, whimpering. Nellie patted her back and made shushing sounds, like a soft breeze. She placed an arm across Hakáta's back and kept petting her. They remained silent for the rest of the ride.

Once they were home, Nellie and Hakáta sat on the front porch steps. Looking out the kitchen window, Martin watched Nellie again place an arm around Hakáta and sing a melody that White Wolf had taught her. *Hey-ya-ya-ya, hey-ya-ya-ya.* It seemed to soothe Hakáta. She finally stopped whimpering.

Martin decided he needed her comfort too. He went out to the front porch and quietly sat down beside them. "Did I ever tell you how White Wolf saved my life?"

Nellie shook her head.

"It happened when I worked for Andrew Sanborn. When I trailed cattle, I was often alone until I came back to camp at day's end. Sometimes I had the feeling someone or something was watching me, but I didn't feel threatened. Then one afternoon, when I was perched on a boulder eating some hardtack, a bullet hit the rock near my knee. I flew off the rock and looked back to see a dead rattlesnake. When I looked in the direction the bullet had come from, who do you think I saw?"

"Was it White Wolf?"

"Yes. That's a good deduction."

"What's that?"

"It means you have a very good mind."

Nellie smiled. "Then what happened?"

"When he started walking toward me, I raised my palm to greet him, then pointed to myself and said 'Handshoe.' He pointed to his chest, said his name in Lakota, and then said, 'White Wolf.'

"I asked him if he knew English. He said, 'Some.' His horse was perfectly trained. He was hidden behind bushes, waiting for a signal from White Wolf to tell him to move. When I pointed to hoofprints and said I was tracking a steer, he pointed across the creek and upstream, showing me where to look for the steer.

"Next I introduced him to Blaze. Of course, Blaze took to him immediately. Then I pulled out some hardtack from my saddlebag and handed it to him. I also gave him my tobacco pouch. I had nothing else to give him for saving my life. After that, White Wolf and I sometimes hunted and went fishing together. We seldom talked a lot, but I very much enjoyed his company."

In March 1889, *The Black Hills Pioneer* reported that, in the fall, North Dakota, South Dakota, and Montana would all be admitted as states to the Union. It also reported the latest change in reservation boundaries. The U.S. Congress had just decided to reduce the previous reservation boundaries by another 9,274,669 acres, forcing native families onto smaller acreages on their North Dakota and South Dakota reservations.

Martin shook his head. This meant tribal areas would be split apart and surrounded by settlers on leased land or allotments. The tribes were also stripped of their right to use 58,695,000 acres across the upper Missouri River drainage basin. The U.S. government clearly felt no obligation to abide by the previous treaties it had signed. He hadn't seen White Wolf since last September and was deeply concerned about him.

Their crow Ezekiel had just returned from wherever he spent his winters. Each year the crow contingent was larger and noisier. Martin and Nellie frequently spread a blanket on their front porch and ate outside, a welcome change from long winter nights in the cabin.

On one of those spring evenings, Nellie was watching Ezekiel retrieve breadcrumbs she'd just strewn across their front yard. He still amused her, especially when he slid down boulders after a rain shower.

"Papa, would you every marry again?"

"For heaven's sake, what made you ask that?"

"Well, someday after I become a lawyer, I might not live here. I don't want you to be alone."

"It surprises me that, at eight years of age, you've already decided to be a lawyer and possibly move away from here. However, when you find yourself a husband, I'll consider looking for a woman."

Nellie rolled her eyes at him.

The following spring, in 1890, Martin and Nellie went to Adrianna's gravesite and spread a bouquet of lilacs at the base of the tombstone. Nell also sprinkled some of Adrianna's perennial herbs near the flowers.

"I think Mama likes knowing her herbs and lilacs are still growing."

"I agree. Not only are her plants surviving, but they're healthier each year. Nellie, your mother didn't come to me in a vision this spring. I believe she knows we're on the right path. You are everything a mother could hope for in a daughter, and everything a father could hope for too."

"Papa, remember how the rug near my bed would be in a different position on the anniversary of her passing? That didn't happen this year."

"Does that make you feel sad?"

"No. When I think about it, it makes me feel peaceful. I think her spirit knows we're managing better and that we'll be all right. She knows we will always carry her in our hearts."

Martin was silent for a few moments, then decided he shouldn't be surprised at what Nellie had said. Early on, Rebekah had told him Nellie was more mature than most children her age.

About a month prior, when he had gone to pick up Nellie, Rebekah had pulled him aside. "Martin, I hope you recognize what a bright child Nellie is. Now that she can read, her nose is stuck in a book whenever she's here. She likes historical novels. Sometimes I think they're over her head but, from the questions she asks, I think she comprehends the stories. If there's a word she doesn't understand, she always asks what it means. Has her teacher mentioned anything about this?"

"Not in so many words. She says things come easily to Nellie. She also mentioned that, maybe after the next school year, it might be a good idea for Nellie to skip a grade. What do you think about that? I'm not in a rush for her to finish school."

"My advice is don't concern yourself about that just now. Give her another school year and see where things stand then."

"Do you think it's because, until she started school, she spent almost all her time being around adults?"

"I'm sure that's part of it, but she has a very inquisitive mind." Rebekah had smiled.

Blaze whinnied somewhat urgently, breaking Martin's train of thought.

"Papa, I think Blaze is tired of waiting for us at the fence. We should head home."

"I think so too. He wants to be in the back pasture."

When they were walking back to the cemetery gate, Nellie said, "Papa, I miss White Wolf. Do you think about him?"

"I think of him every day and am very concerned about him. We haven't seen him in two years. I have no idea which band he might be with. I pray that he's still alive."

After school started in September, Nellie alternated between going to Martin's office or spending a few hours with Rebekah. After her third week of school, she burst through the door to Martin's office. "Papa, a new doctor is taking over for Dr. Laughlin. It's a woman. I think it's time for my checkup."

Martin laughed. "Your checkup isn't due for at least a month or two. Besides, you're healthy as can be. However, if you'd like to give the doctor a nice welcome, you could pick some flowers from our garden and take them to her. Also, there are some wildflowers behind the office."

"That's a good idea. I'll pick some flowers for her and take Hakáta with me."

After about ten minutes, Nellie returned with a big handful of flowers. "What should we put them in?"

Martin walked to the back room of the office and returned with a porcelain pitcher. "I think this will work."

Nellie arranged the flowers. "Let's take them to her now."

Martin sighed. He wasn't excited about making this flower delivery but felt he couldn't refuse her. He hadn't seen her this excited since White Wolf's last visit. The medical office was just down the street. When Nellie ran up to the office door and knocked, Martin stood a few feet behind her.

"Good afternoon. If you came here to see the doctor, I must say you don't look very sick. I'm Dr. Laura Wyatt."

"I'm Nellie Handshoe. This is my father, Martin Handshoe. He's a lawyer. We stopped by to welcome you to Spearfish. And this is Hakáta, my wolf sister." Nellie handed the flowers to Laura.

"Well, what a lovely family. Thank you very much for the

warm welcome. The flowers are beautiful."

Martin removed his hat. "I'm sure you must be busy setting up your office. Perhaps we could come back some other time. As you can see, Nellie is very excited about having a female doctor in town. I expect that goes for most of the women here."

"Thank you for your kind words. I'm very pleased about opening a practice here. As for you three, please stop by again, even if you're not sick. I think we can dispense with formalities. Please call me Dr. Laura." She winked at Nellie.

"Thank you. I will be back soon." Nellie smiled and waved goodbye. Martin nodded and put his hat back on.

After they returned to the office, Nellie curled up in an armchair and started reading a library book. She was humming. Martin smiled to himself. Nellie was lost in her own world and looked very happy.

"Nellie, you look quite content. What are you thinking about?"

"Having Dr. Laura here makes me happy."

"And just why is that?"

"Well, I am glad I won't have to see old Doc Smith for anything personal. I would much rather talk to a woman about private things."

Martin was surprised at her response but then realized that, with no mother to guide her, it made perfect sense. As for himself, his first impression of Dr. Laura was positive. She looked like someone Nellie could trust to give her accurate information. Also, he expected that a younger doctor would be up to date with current medical advancements. It was time for Doc Smith to enjoy his retirement.

Martin was trying to concentrate on a case he'd accepted that morning, but he couldn't stop thinking about Dr. Laura. The instant he laid eyes on her, he had the strangest sensation he'd seen her before. He went to make a cup of tea to distract himself. This often worked for him with cases when something was tugging at the edge of his mind. By the time he finished the tea, he usually had the answer he was seeking.

He took his time drinking the tea and casually watching people walk past the front window. Then it came to him where he'd seen her. About a month ago, an intense dream awakened him shortly before dawn. A woman was asking him for directions. Someone he'd never seen before. And now the woman was here, except Dr. Laura wasn't asking for directions.

This kind of thing hadn't happened to him in years. Sometimes he'd get information through dreams that were vivid enough to awaken him. Usually they were related to legal cases. Several times the information concerned cases he wasn't aware of, cases that lay ahead in the future. The visions occurred often enough that he trusted the information he received.

The last time this had occurred was five years ago, just before Adrianna's passing. He was thankful for the return of this gift. Although foreknowledge could sometimes be painful, he felt it was better than never having intuitions or dreams about the future. They had occurred most of his life, and they usually grounded him.

As for Dr. Laura, he wasn't sure what to think. She'd been very pleasant to them and hadn't seemed the least concerned about having a wolf in her office. He wondered why her spirit had appeared to him in a dream. If it was important enough, he trusted the meaning of the dream would reveal itself. He gave thanks these visions were returning.

Several weeks later, Martin had a legal consultation in Deadwood. When the meeting ended sooner than expected, he stopped by *The Black Hills Pioneer* to have a chat with Karl Johnson, the editor.

"Good morning, Martin. Ever since I received your letter,

I've been wondering what you wanted to talk about. Do we need privacy or would you like to go to a café?"

"Good morning, Karl. I'd prefer to stay here. We might need to search for some information in your old copies."

Johnson signaled for Martin to pull up a chair across the desk from him. "Now, just what is it you'd like to talk about?"

"Would you please tell me what you know about the Ghost Dance the Lakota are practicing? I expect you have more information about this than anyone else I know. I'm trying to sort out fact from rumor. When I stop at the café each morning to have a cup of coffee, the discussion eventually turns to the Ghost Dancing that's taking place on the reservations. The government, settlers, and ranchers are more than unnerved by it. They see it as another reason to extinguish the native way of life. None of it bears well for the Lakota."

"Well, what do you think about it?" Johnson leaned forward in his chair, folded his hands, and set them on his desk.

"First of all, I understand why people are alarmed by it, but I see another side to the Ghost Dancing. I believe it's an act of desperation. So much has been stripped from the tribes—their children, culture, land, the ability to make a livelihood on the plains. Because of the boarding schools, most of them don't see their children for years. With each treaty, more land is stripped from them. There were once more than thirty million buffalo, their main food source. Now there are only a few hundred left near the Canadian border. The tribes relied on them for food and shelter. Their teepees were made from buffalo skins. Now all they have is canvas.

"I've mentioned my Lakota friend to you before. White Wolf saved my life years ago, and my daughter regards him as her grandfather. Because of my friendship with him, I don't accept all the negative things I hear about the Lakota. I want to know what you think, not just about the Ghost Dancing, but where all this is headed."

After his assistant brought them coffee, Johnson closed

the office door and pulled out some files from a cabinet. "I assume you know this is the second Ghost Dance movement. The first one started in 1869 in Nevada. The founder of that ritual was Wodziwob, a Northern Paiute who was known as a healer. He claimed to receive revelations when he was in a trance state.

"After one of those trances, he claimed it had been revealed to him that Natives could create a new paradise by performing certain rituals. He also predicted earthquakes would occur, resulting in a paradise-like world. When the earthquakes didn't occur, people lost faith in his predictions. Interest in his teachings fell off, and he passed away in 1872.

"I need to refer to my notes for this next part. Here's what happened last year on New Year's Day 1889 in Nevada. A Northern Paiute named Wovoka worked on a Nevada ranch from age eight until almost thirty. The owners, David and Abigail Wilson, were devout Christians and introduced Wovoka to the Bible and Christian beliefs. He was cutting wood near the Walker Reservation when a solar eclipse occurred.

"During the eclipse, Wovoka went into a trance and had a vision. He found himself in heaven. He said his ancestors appeared to him, alive and looking well. He claimed God had instructed him to not fight with the white man but to work with him instead. He prophesied the end of white man's expansion in native territories and called for people to dance the same ritual dance that Wodziwob had called for. Wovoka said those who did this would be rewarded in the next life.

"This occurred while the region was experiencing a severe drought. People were desperate to believe in just about anything that might change their circumstances. Whites and natives danced together in the Paiute version of the dance. People came from great distances to hear Wovoka speak. It has been said that he had a dignified presence.

"As his reputation spread, many tribes traveled to hear him speak, including some Lakota who went there last year. When the Lakota brought the Ghost Dance back home, they gave it a different interpretation. They claimed the dance would bring about the resurrection of their ancestors and the return of the buffalo and their land. It was supposed to make the white people disappear.

"This version of the dance spread quickly across the plains. Some of the dancers wrap American flags around themselves, wearing them upside down. The ceremonies can last as long as two days, some even longer. The dancers fast the entire time they're dancing, then fall into trances or drop over from exhaustion. The Ghost Dancers are looking for a different life from that of the reservation. Some of the Lakota dancers wear buckskin shirts with painted designs on them. They call them holy shirts and believe the shirts will protect them from gunshots.

"The Ghost Dance is not a war dance, but settlers, especially those who own property near reservation land, are very concerned about the dancing. People around here are nervous. And I think they have reason to be." Karl folded his hands together and looked at Martin.

"I understand that, Karl. I appreciate your time. It's almost noon. Could I treat you to dinner before I head back to Spearfish? I'd like to talk to you about a case I'm thinking of accepting."

"A free dinner is fine with me. Let's go to the Vienna Restaurant."

As they were about to leave Johnson's office, his assistant handed him a telegram. He quickly perused it and took it with him when they left. "Martin, this will make for an interesting dinner discussion. Two days ago, on December fifteenth, Sitting Bull was killed on the Standing Rock reservation."

As soon as they sat down, Martin said, "Please tell me what happened to Sitting Bull."

"I assume you know he and his followers escaped to Canada after the Battle of the Little Bighorn. They stayed there four years but living conditions were very bad for him and his people. After Sitting Bull surrendered to the U.S. government in 1883, he and his group were assigned to the Standing Rock reservation. It lies northeast of here and abuts the North Dakota border.

"The telegram says that government agents were concerned the Ghost Dance movement could lead to an uprising. A government agent sent Lakota police to arrest Sitting Bull at his cabin. When he refused to leave, a crowd gathered and the police felt threatened. After one of the policemen was shot at, the police shot Sitting Bull in the head and chest. By the end of the gunfight, twelve Hunkpapa were killed and three were wounded."

On December 29, Martin picked up Nellie from school at noon. Another snowstorm was predicted to blow in, and he didn't want to risk getting caught in it. When they arrived at the cabin, Hakáta was pacing on the front porch. She usually stayed in the barn until they came home. She looked upset.

Martin started a fire as soon as they entered the cabin. Hakáta remained near the front door, whimpering. They both tried to console her, but nothing worked. That evening, Nellie brought out two heavy blankets and slept near Hakáta.

In the middle of the night, Martin was awakened by an owl hooting repeatedly. White Wolf had once told him that owls can deliver messages. The longer he listened to it, the more he knew it didn't bode well.

11

WHEN MARTIN WENT TO VALLEY CAFÉ ON JANUARY 2, 1891, the owner told him a massacre had occurred on December 29 at Wounded Knee Creek. Because of the three-day snowstorm, details of the event were only now being reported. *The Black Hills Pioneer* ran a short piece about the battle, stating that details were still coming in.

Within the following week, Martin's worst fears were confirmed when the newspapers reported that over three hundred Lakota, most of them women and children, had been killed at Wounded Knee by the U.S. Cavalry. The list of the victims included White Wolf. When he read the article, Martin was alone in his office. Extremely upset, he pounded his fist against the wall behind his desk.

The next day, his hand looked infected, so he went to see Dr. Laura. The only other time he'd come to her office for a medical reason was when Nellie was running a high fever and had a bad cough. When he entered her office, she was sitting behind her desk.

She took one look at his hand and said, "What happened?"

"I injured it when I was chopping wood."

"Hmmm. It took a tremendous impact to scrape and bruise your hand like this. It will take some time for this to heal."

He winced when she turned his hand over and then looked into his eyes. She clearly suspected he wasn't being truthful.

"It will sting when I clean the cuts. Until they heal, you

must keep your hand bandaged to prevent infection. Use this salve every day. If any infection develops, come see me immediately."

Martin had always thought she was an attractive woman and assumed some of the single men in town were pursuing her. Something about her manner today made him look at her more intently. When she grasped his hand to search for small splinters, she looked so earnest that his heart skipped a beat.

"How is Nellie? I haven't seen her in a while. Sometimes she stops by to say hello."

"Thank you for asking. Just the other day, she said she wants to be a lawyer. She's only in third grade, so we'll see if she actually sticks with that decision. On the other hand, she's a determined little girl. If she decides to pursue this, she'll see it through."

"Your face brightens when you talk about her. I find it interesting that Hakáta meets her at school and walks her to your office. I have never seen a bond like that between a dog and its mistress."

"Do you know the story of how Nellie found Hakáta?"

"She mentioned you two were walking when she heard a crying sound and saw the wolf cub. Then she noticed the mother was dead. That's all she said."

"There were spots of blood in the snow. The mother had been shot. Did she tell you I was opposed to bringing the cub home?"

Dr. Laura shook her head.

"Nellie was so upset that I finally relented. She insisted on saving the cub and said she wouldn't leave unless the cub came with us. I was taken aback by her determination. I told her we'd give it a try, but if the cub had already acquired a taste for wild meat, we couldn't keep her.

"I should have recognized she understood the cub was without a mother, just like she was. As it turns out, she did the right thing about being so insistent. Nellie regards Hakáta as a sister. And I believe Hakáta regards herself as Nellie's protector. She assumed this role so gradually that I didn't quite realize the shift was happening. Then one day something occurred that made it abundantly clear."

"Well, don't leave me hanging. What happened?"

"Has Nellie mentioned our Lakota friend, White Wolf?"

"No, but I'm aware you have a Lakota friend."

"White Wolf was the one who suggested the name to Nellie. Hakáta means 'little sister of a girl.' However, she's much more than that. She is Nellie's protector. And White Wolf was like a grandfather to Nellie."

"What do you mean 'was' like a grandfather?"

"He was killed in the massacre at Wounded Knee."

"When did you learn of his death?"

"Yesterday, when I talked to the editor of the *Spearfish Daily Bulletin*. He was still reviewing information about the massacre and said he plans to run the story tomorrow. He was going over the lists of those killed on both sides. I could tell he was reluctant to show the lists to me. He knew White Wolf and I were friends."

"I'm so very sorry, Martin."

"I'll have to tell Nellie about it tonight. I need to prepare her. Once the article is published, she'll hear about it at school. I'm sure you know there's mixed sentiment about natives, not only here but across the country. Many people I know think it was all right for our government to violate its treaties and seize land that had been guaranteed to the tribes.

"The day the massacre occurred, Hakáta was very distressed. When we came home late that afternoon, she was pacing back and forth across our porch. She usually spends the day in the barn or close to it. She came inside with us but remained near the front door, whimpering. Nellie finally threw some blankets down and slept next to her that night. I don't understand how, but Hakáta knew White Wolf had been killed."

Laura shook her head in sympathy. "After you tell Nellie, if I could be of help, don't hesitate to let me know. You're welcome to bring Hakáta too."

He watched Dr. Laura purse her lips, take another look at his hand, and draw the correct conclusion about his injury. She kept her thoughts to herself, which he appreciated. He knew from his loss of Adrianna that deep wounds of the heart don't heal quickly, if ever.

"You must keep the dressing clean. If it needs to be dressed again or if the pain doesn't decrease in a couple of days, come back so I can check for infection. You're left-handed, aren't you?"

Martin nodded.

"Well, it's a good thing you didn't injure that hand."

He stopped at the front door and turned around. She was still looking at him.

"Martin, don't let your rage consume you. Forge it into something else."

He started to leave, then thought better of it and leaned back in. "Thank you."

"You're quite welcome."

After supper that evening, Martin asked Nellie to sit near the fireplace with him. "Nellie, the newspapers have reported more information about the killings at Wounded Knee. Today, as best as they could determine, they printed the names of those who were killed there."

"I know what you're going to tell me. Hakáta told us the night she wouldn't stop crying near the front door." Hearing her name, Hakáta came across the room and Nellie moved down to the rug. She petted Hakáta with one hand and brushed away tears with the other.

Martin moved from his rocking chair to the rug, placed

an arm around Nellie, and rested a hand on Hakáta's back. Thinking back to the day of the massacre, Martin remembered Nellie coming to the office after school. She'd seemed out of sorts, which was unusual for her. When they got home, Hakáta was restless, begging to go outside and then wanting to come back in. On some level, they had both sensed something was wrong—they just didn't know what.

The following day, *The Black Hills Pioneer* published more details about the massacre. Martin read everything before settling down to work. The lead article stated that an inexperienced agent had recently been assigned responsibility for the Pine Ridge Reservation. When he saw the Lakota wearing Ghost Dance shirts, he panicked and requested a thousand troops be sent to restore order on the reservation. By mid-November, the Pine Ridge and Rosebud Reservations were surrounded by cavalry.

During this time, Sitting Bull returned from Canada with his tribe. On December 15, when tribal police tried to arrest him, Sitting Bull was killed. The remaining 200 members of his band joined Spotted Elk's band, who, after they learned of Sitting Bull's death, tried to escape to the Badlands. The band stood at about 300 Lakota, most of them women and children. When a winter storm blew in, they were forced to head back toward the Pine Ridge Reservation. After they encountered U.S. troops, Spotted Elk raised a white flag and surrendered. His band was then ordered to camp five miles west of Wounded Knee Creek, where it was surrounded by the U.S. 7th Cavalry Regiment.

On the morning of December 29, the U.S. Cavalry went into the camp to disarm the Lakota. While they were seizing weapons, a rifle was fired and the troops started shooting. It was unclear which side fired the first rifle shot. Some of the

Lakota fired back but many had already been stripped of their weapons. By the time the battle was over, roughly twenty-five soldiers were dead, and more than 250 Lakota had been killed, mostly women and children.

Martin threw the newspaper down on his desk. The article didn't refer to it as a massacre, but that's what it was. As he thought about it, he realized it had occurred the same day Hakáta had been pacing their porch and whining when he and Nellie came home from work.

That following spring in 1891, Martin and Nellie rode to the spot where they had last seen White Wolf. Hakáta sat between them on the buckboard seat, ever vigilant for any prey or danger. The previous evening they'd made prayer ties, stuffing tobacco in little cloth sacks and tying them shut with string. When they reached the pine tree where White Wolf had separated from them, they knelt and tied the sacks onto the lower branches.

"Nellie, would you like to say something, or do you want your thoughts to remain private?"

Nellie called Hakáta to her side. "I will say something. Tuŋkášila, we are here to honor you. I miss you and will carry you in my heart forever. So will Hakáta. The soldiers killed my grandpa. They killed babies and children. They killed mothers and old men."

Then she untied the ribbons at the ends of her braids and tied them to a low branch, letting them hang like the other prayer strips. Hakáta threw her head back and howled.

The plaintive howl tore into Martin's heart. He wasn't sure how long it continued. When he felt Nellie's hand on his shoulder, he turned to look at her. Her other hand was on Hakáta's back. There were no tears on her face. She looked strong, as if looking to the future when she could channel this atrocity into some form of justice.

Martin took a deep breath. "White Wolf, we will never forget your presence in our lives. I will always carry your memory in my heart."

On the way home, Nellie looked over at him. "Papa, let's come here every year to honor White Wolf."

Martin nodded. "Yes, we will do that. At least once a year."

"Hakáta knows what happened."

"Yes, she does. She is more intelligent than half the people I know."

Nellie looked over at him and smiled.

"We came here to honor White Wolf and show our respect for him. He saved my life. If not for him, I would never have met your mother, and you wouldn't be my daughter. I cannot imagine life without you."

She looked at him with tear-rimmed eyes.

A week after their journey to honor White Wolf, shortly after sunrise, Nellie ran into the kitchen. "Papa, come see the rug by my bed."

Martin set down his coffee mug and followed Nellie to her bedroom.

"Look. The fringes have been braided. It's the way Tuŋkášila taught me to braid."

"Yes, it is. What do you think about this?"

"I think his spirit is watching over us."

"I agree. I've never seen anything like this."

In March 1892, local newspapers reported that a measles epidemic was spreading through the Black Hills. With Nellie's school closed for at least a week, Rebekah had insisted on watching her while Martin was at work. There were warnings of a possible snowstorm over the weekend, so Martin closed the office early Friday afternoon.

When he stopped by the McGranes' to get Nellie, Rebekah pulled him inside. "Something is wrong with Nellie. I'm concerned she might have contracted measles. She just started coughing and has a runny nose. I think you should take her to Dr. Laura. Here's a blanket for you."

Martin quickly wrapped the blanket around Nellie. "Several of her schoolmates have been kept home because of it. I'll let you know what Dr. Laura thinks it is."

He carried Nellie to their buggy and urged Blaze to run as fast as possible. When they reached Laura's office, Martin didn't bother to hitch up Blaze. He just burst through the office door carrying Nellie.

Laura took one look at her. "Follow me to the exam room. Nellie, are you able to sit up or would you prefer to lie down? I need to take your temperature and examine you."

"I want to lie down."

"Your temperature is just over 100. I can see a light rash on your face. I think you have measles, and I'm hoping it will be a mild case. Martin, if it's all right with you, I'd like to spend the night at Nellie's bedside in case the snowstorm makes travel difficult."

"I'd appreciate that very much. You may ride home with us. I'll bring you back to your office whenever you need."

Laura nodded and pulled on her winter coat. "I just need to get my medical kit." She held Nellie close to her while they rode to the cabin. "Do you know if Adrianna ever had measles?"

"Yes, she did. And I had them when I was eight years old."

"Were you very sick?"

"I had a bad cough and absolutely no appetite. I remember one of my brothers laughing at my red eyes. I'll leave you and Nellie at the house and then put Blaze in the barn. It's going to be a very frigid night."

When he entered the cabin, Laura had already placed some blankets near the fireplace for her and Nellie. "I want to stay close to Nellie and monitor her through the night. I can sleep lightly. I've done this watch many times. I'll listen for any change in her breathing and let you know if she takes a turn for the worse. Which, by the way, I'm not expecting. You need to get as much sleep as possible."

Martin checked on Nellie and Laura twice during the night. The second time, Laura looked up at Martin from the blankets. When she started to raise herself, Martin motioned for her to stay put and knelt on the floor.

"Nellie's fever broke about an hour ago. I gave her liquids several times, and she has kept everything down. She is not out of the woods, but I'm sure this will not be a severe case of the virus. It's just four o'clock. Let me sleep another two hours." Laura sank back into the pillow and rolled over.

At six o'clock, Martin knelt and touched Laura's shoulder. "I just made some coffee. I'll be at the kitchen table."

A few minutes later, Laura tiptoed over to the table.

"Could you stay for a cup of coffee before I take you home?"

Laura nodded, looking sleepy. "Nellie is going to be all right, but she will not have her normal strength for at least a week. With some people it takes longer than that. I assume Rebekah will watch her."

"Yes, she will, and I'll bring her home early every day. I can't thank you enough for staying here last night. Knowing Nellie couldn't be in better hands allowed me to get some sleep. I just need a few minutes to hitch up Blaze."

"Nellie is sleeping deeply. She'll be fine while you take me home."

A week later, when Nellie was back in school, Martin followed through on a decision he'd given great consideration. Just before noon, he closed his office and walked down the street to talk to Laura. With six inches of new fallen snow, the town looked freshly scrubbed.

Laura had now been in Spearfish for three years. Until last night, Martin had assumed that one of the town's wealthy bachelors was probably courting her. However, after Laura's overnight stay in their home, he wondered if perhaps she actually wasn't spending time with anyone. He decided it was time to find out.

When he looked through the office door, he didn't see any patients, but he also didn't see her. He took a deep breath and opened the door. "Laura, are you here?"

Laura responded from her private living area, "Martin, just give me a moment. This is a surprise. I was about to lock the door and take a noon break. Are you feeling all right?"

"Yes, I think so. I've been wondering if you would like to have dinner with Nellie and me sometime."

She looked surprised. "I would enjoy that."

"I don't want to create an awkward situation if you're committed to someone else."

"You wouldn't be interfering with anything. It would be nice to have dinner with you two. Nellie's a remarkable girl, and you are quite an interesting man."

Martin looked down for a moment. He felt sure he was blushing. "Well, if you get to know me better, you might not find me so interesting." Then he looked straight into her eyes and liked what he saw.

She studied him intently for a few moments. "Are you thinking that I want to find a wealthy husband? I had one, and that was the most difficult time of my life. He was a lawyer, and not a very honest one.

"Sometimes instead of growing in love, the love between a couple withers. It doesn't happen quickly. It can take a while to comprehend, but one day you wake up and realize there's a deep chasm between you and your mate; that the love you once shared is gone. It's painful to come to terms with."

Martin wondered why she was so defensive. "Am I to assume you don't take kindly to lawyers?"

Laura laughed. "Well, let's just say they have to prove themselves to me."

"Ever since I met you, I've wondered what made you decide to move to Spearfish."

"That's a long story and better told at another time. I need to get back to work."

"I have one request before I leave. Sometime, would you please talk to Nellie and explain the physical changes she'll soon be going through? I gave her a book that explains it, but I'm sure she wouldn't feel comfortable asking me any questions about it. I also think Nellie is afraid of dying like Adrianna did. She says she doesn't want to have children. The mother of one of her classmates died recently giving birth to her sixth child. I think it would help her if she could talk to you about her concerns."

"Of course I would do that, Martin. Just tell her to stop by my office sometime. I'll be guided by her reactions and let her control the conversation. Also, I have a book or two she may take home with her. I'll let you know how our chat goes, but I won't reveal anything she doesn't want me to."

"One more thing. She seems to be pulling back from me a bit."

"That is very normal for her age."

Several days later, Martin looked through Laura's office window to make sure no one was in her waiting area. He rang the doorbell, knowing it was close to her noon break.

After a few seconds, she came from her apartment and unlocked the front door. "Come in, Martin. Are you all right?"

"Yes. I apologize for disrupting your break. I just think it's the best time for us to talk without being disturbed. I wanted you to know that Nellie seems more at ease since your discussion with her. Thank you for the books you loaned her. She's been reading them in her bedroom. It's ridiculous that I wasn't thinking ahead about her developing into a young woman."

"Maybe you're not ready for her to grow up and possibly move away."

"I expect you're right. I'll try to do better. Also, for the first time, we talked at length about Adrianna's death. She was only four years old when Adrianna passed. Nellie told me everything she remembers. I admitted to her how devastating it was for me to lose Adrianna and Nellie's baby sister. I hadn't realized how much pain I've been carrying inside me. Through helping her, you're also helping me. I thank you on both counts.

"One more thing. I was wondering if you'd like to have supper with Nellie and me tomorrow. After school she studies and sometimes goes to a friend's house, but she is always at my office by five o'clock. We usually go to The Breakfast House around six o'clock for supper." His hands were sweaty. He studied Laura's face for any indication of unease but didn't detect any.

"Martin, it would be a pleasure to do that. Thank you."

The following evening, Martin and Nellie stopped by Laura's office, and the three of them walked to The Breakfast House. Martin nodded to his friends and clients who were there. He noticed that nobody looked surprised to see the threesome. Laura kept the conversation moving, asking far-ranging questions about Nellie and Martin's interests other than law.

The evening passed quickly. After he and Nellie walked Laura home, it was clear they would be meeting for supper on a very regular basis. Martin felt a lightness of heart that he hadn't experienced for a very long time.

In late May 1894, Martin was poring over a case file when Nellie burst into his office. "You said we could take a train to Cheyenne when school was finished. This was my last day of school until September. When could we leave?"

Martin laughed. "Actually, I had a telegram from James this morning confirming the dates for our visit. We'll leave this Friday and spend a week there. You'll have all day tomorrow to pack your suitcase. I just arranged for someone to check on the house and make sure Blaze and Hakáta are all right."

"Where will we stay?"

"I made a reservation at a small hotel near Main Street, not far from James's home. Also, I just sent a telegram to Doc Matheson asking him if we could ride out to see him. I'd like for him to meet you and for you to see his ranch."

"Thank you, Papa. I'm so excited."

Nellie was now twelve years old, but to Martin it seemed she acted older than that. The years were passing too quickly for him.

Their train left early Friday morning. Martin hadn't seen Nellie this animated in a very long time. She asked to sit next to the window and, other than eating in the dining car, stayed glued to her seat. The shifting landscape held her captive the entire trip.

After arriving late that afternoon, they went straight to the hotel. When they checked in, the clerk handed Martin two envelopes. One was a note from James inviting them to supper that evening, saying it was about a fifteen-minute walk to their home. The other was from Doc Matheson, giving

Martin his telephone number and inviting them to spend a couple of nights at his ranch. Martin immediately rang Doc and arranged to visit him in two days. Doc insisted on having Jake bring them to the ranch.

After they unpacked, they started walking to James's home.

"Papa, don't walk so fast. I want to see what kind of shops there are in Cheyenne."

"All right, I'll slow down. See that sign for Connors General Store? That's James's store. When the previous owner decided to retire, he accepted James's offer to buy the business."

"Where is the law office you worked for?"

"It's in the next block. They just never had enough work to hire me full-time. In the end, it all worked out. Otherwise I would never have met Adrianna or have you for my daughter. It's intriguing how life works."

When they arrived at James and Anna's home, the boys flew out the door before Martin had a chance to knock.

James stepped out onto the porch, shaking his head. "They're very excited to talk to Nellie about her pet wolf."

"Samuel and Nathan, come here and say hello to your Uncle Martin."

After Nellie met Anna and James, the boys insisted that she join them on the back porch until it was time for supper. They wanted to hear all about Hakáta and the Black Hills. Martin, James, and Anna sat at the kitchen table, amused and pleased the back porch conversation was going so well.

The next day, Martin showed Nellie around Cheyenne. After spending some time in James's store, they walked to the law firm where Martin had done contract work. When they entered the office, Michael McCann immediately recognized him.

"Well, Martin Handshoe. Nice to see you. It's been a long time."

"Yes, it has." Martin shook McCann's hand and introduced him to Nellie.

"How long will you be in town?"

"Until next Friday."

"How about meeting for dinner tomorrow at Ford Restaurant? James told me you have a law office in Spearfish. I'd like to hear about it."

"We'll see you then. I trust it's fine if Nellie joins us. She is quite determined to read the law."

"Well, that's commendable. Miss Nellie, you let us know if you ever move to Cheyenne. See you at noon tomorrow."

That evening, James's boys and Nellie had an animated conversation about Cheyenne and what they wanted to pursue after twelfth grade. Martin could see Nellie's brain working hard. An image of her residing in Cheyenne flashed through his mind.

When they stepped outside the hotel the next morning, Jake was standing beside the ranch wagon. Martin and Jake regarded each other for a few moments, taking in the changes time had wrought, then clasped each other's shoulders.

Jake helped Nellie onto the wagon seat. "So you're the famous Miss Nellie I've been hearing about."

"Yes, and I've heard a lot about you too. I have wanted to meet you for a long time."

"Martin, we've had some heavy rains. Be on the lookout for washouts."

Nellie sat quietly between Martin and Jake, taking in the landscape. Martin wondered what she was thinking, then realized he already knew. She was being seduced by Wyoming.

Doc was reading the paper on his front porch when they arrived. Martin was impressed with Doc's physical condition. Only his white hair gave a hint of his age.

"Come on in. I'll show you to your bedrooms. My wife is visiting her sister in Nebraska. You'll have to come back and see Etta some other time. When you come downstairs, I'll give you a walking tour. We've made a few changes since you left, Martin. And Miss Nellie, just how good a horseback rider are you?"

"I'm good. Sometimes Papa and I go for long rides. I also go hunting with him to keep him company."

"Well, how about Jake giving you a horseback tour of the ranch tomorrow?"

"Thank you very much. I'd like that."

The next day, while Jake showed Nellie the ranch, Martin and Doc had coffee on the front porch.

"Doc, I apologize for leaving the ranch so abruptly."

"Martin, I knew Etta's nephew was trouble from the day he landed here. I regret not making him leave before you were forced to flee for your safety. I rode into town shortly after you left and had a long talk with James. He explained everything to me. Life is interesting. I'm not sure if I believe in fate, but an unfortunate incident—whether caused by accident or by fate—can force a person to change the direction of their life. You would never have met Adrianna and have this wonderful daughter if you hadn't left here."

"I agree. I have an incident to relate that reinforces what you just said. Shortly after Sanborn established his ranch, I was out on the range tracking down some cattle. Around noon I settled myself on a big boulder to eat some hardtack. Just before I took a bite, a bullet hit close to me. I jumped off the boulder, only to see a dead rattlesnake at my feet and a Lakota heading my way.

"After that, I'd see him every once in a while on the ranch, and we became friends. When I moved to Spearfish to practice law, he'd stop by my cabin every so often and sleep on the front porch. We often went fishing and hunting. I will always feel indebted to him for saving my life. Nellie regards him as her grandfather.

"He brought us great comfort after Adrianna's passing.

In the mid-1880s, his family was forced off the land where they'd always lived. Then in 1890 he was killed in the massacre at Wounded Knee Creek. Every year, Nellie and I ride to the meadow where we last saw him to honor his memory. I will always carry him in my heart."

"I'm sorry, Martin. The Federal Government has broken one treaty after another. There's no defending their failure to honor the treaty terms they signed with the tribes."

"I don't know many people who feel that way."

After supper, Doc, Nellie, and Martin sat on a blanket in the front yard and watched the sunset. With no clouds obscuring the night sky, the three stargazers spent the rest of the evening searching for constellations. Martin pointed out the Watanka constellation, the variation of the Big Dipper that White Wolf had shown him and Adrianna.

Their visit to Cheyenne passed quickly, like scudding clouds that race with the wind. The day before they were to return home, Martin hired a horse and rode out to Doc's ranch.

"Martin, this is a nice surprise. I didn't think I'd see you again before you left."

"Nellie is spending the day with James's sons, so it gave me a chance to see you one more time. She is quite taken with Cheyenne. Frankly, it wouldn't surprise me if she moves here when she finishes school. She's determined to have the right to vote."

"Well, from the short amount of time I've spent with her, she also seems determined to establish herself as a lawyer. Being the state capital, Cheyenne would offer her more opportunities than Spearfish."

"Yes, it would. I'd never try to hold her back. She's gaining a sense of her future. The first time I stepped into a law office with my father, I was intrigued with the concept of practicing law. I think Nellie will follow the same path.

"If she doesn't stay in Spearfish, that's her decision. I want her to follow her dreams. I brought her here to meet individuals from my past who remain important to me. As it turns out, meeting these friends has made her think even more about her future. I wasn't expecting that."

"If Nellie moves to Cheyenne at some point, would you consider returning back here?"

"I'd have to think long and hard about that. Right now it's out of the question. I can't walk away from my law practice, but I could visit here on a regular basis. It's been an incredible pleasure to see you again."

"I hope you and Nellie will find time to come to Cheyenne every summer. You're always welcome here."

"We just might take you up on that."

12

THE DAY AFTER THEY RETURNED FROM CHEYENNE,
Martin stopped by Laura's office. "I was wondering if you
could have supper with us tonight."

"Yes, I could. Thank you."

"We'll stop by after work. Nellie wants to tell you all about
the trip and so do I. One more thing. Are you aware we're a
topic of discussion by some townspeople?"

"By townspeople I assume you're referring to a couple of
elderly busybodies that people try to stay away from."

"That's correct."

"I think we should ignore them. I don't believe people give
them any credence. I'm steeping tea. Would you like some?"

"Yes. Thank you." He sat down at her small dining table
and watched her pour the tea. She always looked earnest about
any task she undertook.

"Now, just what is it you came here to talk about?"

"In general I think that people who live in the western frontier states—like South Dakota, Wyoming, Colorado,
Montana—want their personal independence respected. They
want people to stay out of their business.

"After I left the office yesterday, I stopped by the McGranes'
to pick up Nellie. Rebekah had been helping her with a science
project. She pulled me aside while Nellie continued to work on
her project. She said townspeople are recognizing that your
medical knowledge is more extensive than our previous doc-

tors, especially when it comes to planning for children.

"She also mentioned that a couple of women brought up the Comstock Act when they met to have tea with Rebekah. They discussed the illegality of sending any writings about conception or any instruments for preventing conception through the United States mail. I just want to make sure you're aware of all the ramifications of that law. I don't want you to get into any kind of trouble."

"Thank you for your concern. I studied the Comstock Act as soon as it was passed to make sure I understood all its implications. I've never violated it, but I have found some ways to work around it. The Comstock Act was passed by lawmakers who think that birth control is immoral and obscene. I don't agree with that. I think it was wrong for Comstock to force his puritanical views on the American public. If he were a woman having her eighth or ninth child without sufficient resources to feed all of them, he might feel differently."

"I'm concerned about someone going after you under this act. How have you managed to work around that?"

"First of all, the actual name for it is the Federal Anti-Obscenity Act of 1873. I don't consider the sex act obscene, and I find nothing wrong with couples wanting to have some space between their children. Men and women have been practicing different forms of birth control for centuries.

"As for working around the act, I never use the United States mail to receive any materials that concern sexual development and pregnancy. Nor do I use the mail to receive any contraceptive devices."

"Laura, you need to thread that needle very carefully. I'm quite sure there are a number of residents in this town who support Comstock's position and would be only too glad to enforce it."

"I promise to be careful. I would never receive anything through the United States mail that could be construed as a violation of the act."

"All right, I'll accept that you know what you're doing. I won't question you about this ever again. I just want you to be safe."

In August 1895, Martin and Nellie were standing in their front yard, waiting patiently for the moonrise. After the golden orb appeared above the pine trees, they watched its ascent for a long time.

"Papa, there is something I want to talk about before I go to bed. I've been thinking about Tuŋkášila."

"I'll make some tea for us. I've been thinking about him too."

"Two years ago, when we went close to Wounded Knee to honor his life, something happened to me. I had a vision of the person I want to become."

"Please tell me about your vision."

"I see how Dr. Laura helps people because of her medical knowledge. I would like to do the same but through using the law. I've been thinking more about it since we came back from Cheyenne. Wyoming gave women the right to vote in 1869."

"Yes, I'm aware of that. Does that mean you'd like to live there eventually?"

"Maybe, Papa."

"Would you like to start helping with some basic legal tasks in my office?"

"Yes, please. My homework doesn't take much time."

"Nellie, between your intelligence and your compassion for people, I think you'd make an outstanding lawyer."

On a warm Saturday afternoon in September, Martin, Nellie, and Laura were planning to have a picnic near the creek that ran behind the cabin. Their favorite spot was beneath a big pine that dappled shade across the meadow. Hakáta loved it too. They were just leaving the cabin with their picnic basket when the sheriff came riding fast in their direction. His horse was pulling a small wagon, which was unusual.

The sheriff reined in his horse to a quick stop but stayed in the wagon. "Dr. Laura, I need you to come back to town real fast. Dave Braun was about to enter the café when he grabbed his chest and fell onto the boardwalk. He is alive but breathing real heavy. I know he goes to Doc Smith in Deadwood, but would you please come with me?"

"Yes. Of course I will." Laura started climbing into the sheriff's wagon. "Martin, here's the key to my office. My bag is near the back door. Please bring it to the café."

"Papa, I want to watch Laura and see what she does. Hakáta does too."

"All right. Help me hitch Blaze to the cart."

By the time Martin arrived at The Breakfast House, Braun was in a sitting position, leaning against the building. Laura quickly grabbed her bag and checked Braun's blood pressure and heart rate. Martin heard her give a sigh of relief.

"Mr. Braun, your heart seems fine. Are you on some kind of medication?"

"I've been having a lot of heartburn, so the doc in Deadwood prescribed something for me."

"Well, it's quite possible you've had a strong reaction to the medication. Perhaps the dose was too large or you had an allergic reaction. I advise you to stop taking it and consult your doctor. You might be able to flush it from your system by drinking a lot of water today. Is there someone who could take you home and stay with you through the night?"

"My wife's at home. One of my friends can take me there."

"Don't hesitate to contact me if you have trouble again tonight. You're welcome to stop by my office any time."

Braun nodded. "Thank you, Dr. Laura."

After the crowd broke up, Martin said, "Well, after all that, do you still want to have a picnic?"

"Yes, by all means. Sitting under that beautiful pine in your backyard would be a wonderful way to let down."

"I think you'll be seeing more male patients soon. What you just did for Mr. Braun was very impressive. I watched the crowd gathering around you. I think more than a few of them will no longer be going to Deadwood to see a doctor."

From then on, Laura often joined Martin and Nellie for supper at The Breakfast House. Townspeople were well aware that Martin valued his privacy and that of his clients. Curious as they might be about his seeing Laura, they gave him the personal space he needed.

Now in her sixth year in Spearfish, Laura's practice was flourishing. Because of her gentle manner, children weren't afraid to see her. And, as Martin had predicted, more men were consulting her for medical treatment.

On a frigid February evening, Martin and Laura had supper at the café and then, since Nellie was spending the night with a friend, went to Laura's. She stoked the potbellied stove to heat the small living area and made some tea.

"Laura, something you said tonight reminded me of Adrianna. You were brave to come to Spearfish on your own. I admire you for taking that risk. Adrianna's life was very difficult before she fled here."

"What happened to her?"

"Her parents died when she was sixteen. She had four siblings, and they were all farmed out to live with different relatives. She ended up with her sister who lived on a farm in eastern South Dakota. She was married and had a couple of children. The plan was for Adrianna to help with the children and farm chores. Within a few months it became clear her brother-in-law was very attracted to her. Her sister also recognized it.

"One day Adrianna saw a newspaper ad for a Deadwood bar wanting women to dance with their patrons. The ad said the bar would reimburse women for the stagecoach fare. When she showed it to her sister, her sister gave her enough money to get to Deadwood. That evening, Adrianna fled after sunset. She walked to town and hid herself until she could board the stagecoach the next morning.

"I happened to be in Deadwood just as she was stepping off the coach. When I saw the bar owner heading toward her, I knew exactly what his intentions were. She was striking, with long auburn hair. I knew it would only be a matter of time before the bar owner would expect her to do more than just dance with men.

"So I approached her and told her what I thought he had in mind for her. I offered to take her to Spearfish and assured her that good friends of mine—a minister and his wife—would give her shelter. She took a good look at the bar owner and decided to leave with me. I told her I'd bring her back to Deadwood if she didn't like living in Spearfish.

"Everything went beautifully for several years. Then, when Nellie was three years old, Adrianna went into an early labor with our second child. From the very start her labor was difficult. It was a breech birth, and the baby was too large to turn." Martin looked away, blinking back tears. "I'm embarrassed. I don't know why all this came bursting out of me."

"You have needed to talk to someone about this for a long time. You must understand you were not responsible for her death. Loving and losing is part of our humanity. We cannot control it. It's obvious that you and Adrianna loved each other deeply. Many people don't ever experience that kind of love. She is part of the fabric of your being, even though she passed years ago. Do you understand that? Not every couple grows close enough for that to happen. There is a wedding wish—'May you grow in love.' It's a tremendous blessing when it occurs."

"I've never thought about it like that. There have been times when I needed to tell Nellie something I knew she wouldn't want to hear. Before blurting out anything, I try to think what Adrianna would have said to her. She always got her point across but her gentle manner never provoked a defensive remark. I, on the other hand, am not so good at that."

"I certainly didn't experience anything like that in my marriage," Laura remarked. "I was so focused on becoming a doctor that I didn't have much of a social life. I hoped to marry someday but wanted to have my medical degree first. It turned out that was never a problem because I didn't meet anyone who really appealed to me. Then, in my last year of medical school, I met Stephen. He was in his first year of law practice and was filled with plans for his legal career. He had a good mind. He seemed genuinely interested in wanting to marry me, but maybe it was just wishful thinking on my part. Maybe he just liked the idea of the income I could generate.

"Whatever love there had been between us disappeared within a few years. The marriage became more of a business partnership. He made a respectable income as a lawyer but he also wanted all the income I brought in. If we could have had children, it might have made a difference, but I doubt it. When I said that I wanted to invest some of my income as I saw fit, he was outraged. I thought he was going to hit me. I left several weeks later when he was on a business trip."

"Laura, what do you mean, 'if you could have had children'?"

"When I learned I'd never be able to bear children, I felt a sense of relief. My marriage brought me no joy. I suspected he was unfaithful to me, and I didn't want to be trapped in an empty marriage. Having a child would have made it very difficult to leave, so at least I didn't have to worry about that. I knew deep inside what I needed to do."

"Thank you for being so open. I always treat everything you say in absolute confidence. If you ever think Nellie is interested in someone who has a questionable reputation, I'd appreciate you sharing that experience. She needs to hear a woman's side of things, not just her father warning her about unscrupulous men. She talks about wanting to be a lawyer, so I hope that will keep her from an early marriage. I want her to experience something more than this town before she settles down."

"Martin, she's very clear about wanting to practice law. I don't think she will let anyone or anything get in the way of that. I'm sure she will marry one day. I predict she'll find a very self-assured man who isn't threatened by her."

"I hope you're right. I'll try to hold onto that thought."

In 1895, when Nellie turned thirteen, Martin gave her the amber brooch he'd given to Adrianna when they married. "Happy birthday, Nellie. I've been waiting until your thirteenth birthday to give this to you. I'm not good at wrapping things so I just tied a ribbon around the little package."

"It still looks pretty. Thank you, Papa." She carefully untied the ribbon and opened the box. "What kind of gemstone is on the necklace?"

"It's amber. My grandmother considered it an amulet. Before my family left the Netherlands and sailed to America, she gave this to my mother, Nell, your namesake. Knowing it was a final parting made it very difficult for them to say goodbye. I will never forget how my grandmother embraced my mother, both of them sobbing."

"I like the idea of the amber piece protecting me. For now I'll keep it at my bedside, but I will wear it every day when I start reading the law."

Early the next morning, Martin was fixing oatmeal when Nellie came out of her bedroom.

"Nellie, you're up early today."

"Papa, something unusual happened last night. You know how I always sleep with my bedroom door open? In the middle of the night, I woke up and saw moonlight spreading across my bed, then spilling through my doorway all the way to the kitchen.

"A Lakota brave was standing in the kitchen, looking out the window near the front door. His hair was in a long braid, and he was wearing a buckskin shirt and leggings with fringe. He looked at me for a few moments, then turned around and walked through the wall near the door."

"Did the vision scare you?"

"Not at all. His face was filled with kindness."

"I wonder if that's how White Wolf looked when he was young. Perhaps his spirit is watching over you. He cared so very much for you."

Each day after school, Nellie went to Martin's office to check in with him. She usually stayed there and did schoolwork, then spent the rest of the afternoon with a friend. On a rainy day in early April, she burst into the office. "Papa, I'm going to stay here and do homework. It's too rainy and chilly to go to Miriam's house."

"I've been waiting for you. I have a meeting with our banker. It shouldn't last long."

"Take your time. Hakáta will help me with my homework." Nellie smiled and opened a book.

About ten minutes after Martin sat down with the banker, he felt a sense of panic. "I'm sorry to leave so abruptly. I have a strong feeling something is wrong with Nellie." He grabbed his satchel and flew out the door. Just as he approached his office, a gunshot rang out. He would never forgive himself or God if something happened to Nellie. He threw open the office door and saw Nellie pointing her handgun at a stranger, with Hakáta standing at her side.

At that moment, the owner of the hardware store ran into the office. He looked from Martin to Nellie. "How can I help?"

Martin and Nellie both had their pistols trained on the man. "I just got here," Martin said. "Please get the sheriff."

"I told him to be still or I'd shoot him again, only this time it wouldn't be his hand. I'm all right, Papa, but he isn't. I had to make him drop his gun."

Sheriff McGuire and one of his deputies burst into the office. "What just happened?"

"That man walked into the office just after Papa left for a meeting at the bank. I took one look at him and knew he was trouble. I told him to stop right where he was and head back out the door. When he started walking toward me, I pulled my pistol out of the desk, stood up, and leveled the gun at him.

"I told him again to turn around and leave. He laughed at me, placed his hand on the gun in his holster, and continued coming toward me. I shot his hand before he could pull his gun."

Martin grabbed the man's lower arms while the sheriff pulled out a pair of handcuffs and clamped them on the man's wrists. The man's hand was bleeding, but it wasn't serious.

"Martin, I want you and Nellie to come to my office as soon as I have him behind bars. We need to find out who he is." The sheriff and his deputy grabbed the man by his upper arms and escorted him to the jail.

"We'll be there shortly. Just let me talk to Nellie and find out exactly what occurred." Martin walked over to Nellie's desk, pulled up a chair, and took a deep breath. "Now, tell me what happened."

"When that man walked into the office, I took one look at him and a chill ran down my spine. It happened just after you left so he must have been waiting for you to leave. I had no doubt he was going to attack me."

"I think I recognize him. Roughly five years ago he beat up one of my clients and was charged with assault and attempted robbery. Somehow he managed to escape from the Deadwood jail. I've always wondered if he paid off one of the night staff. Anyway, I had hoped we'd seen the last of him."

Martin's mind was racing. What had that criminal intended to do with Nellie? Kidnap her? Assault her? He wanted to beat the man senseless, but then he'd be charged with assault.

After he and Nellie met with the sheriff, they went to The Breakfast House for their noon meal.

"Nellie, we need to set up some new procedures. I want Hakáta in the office with you if I need to be absent for any reason. If I have to leave even for a few minutes, that door needs to be locked. I'm too upset right now to come up with any other ideas. You think about it too, please."

"Papa, here's one good thing to think about. You know how you sometimes have foreknowledge? Well, the same thing has started to happen with me. I will pay close attention to it."

In early June, Martin arrived at work early. He wanted to catch Laura before she started seeing any patients. When a light went on in her office, he walked across the street.

"Martin, I'm surprised to see you so early."

"I have a busy day ahead. I was wondering if you're free for dinner tonight."

"Yes, I am. What time should I meet you?"

"I'll stop by for you at six o'clock. I have no idea if Nellie will be able to join us."

"Before you leave, Nellie stopped by yesterday and said she had some questions about the sexual education informa-tion I'd given her. We talked for about half an hour. I treated her as a young adult. I just want to make sure that's all right with you."

"That's fine with me. I want her to be as informed as she can possibly be."

"Also, Nellie mentioned she's afraid of dying in childbirth like her mother did, so I told her about a friend's experience. When my friend's mother was twenty-eight years old, she died giving birth to my friend. My friend was a healthy baby and survived just fine. Then years later, on the day my friend turned twenty-nine, she felt a great sense of relief and couldn't understand why. Then she realized that, for all those years after her mother's passing, some part of her mind had expected that she might also die at twenty-eight."

"Thank you for telling Nellie that. I'm sure she'll find that very helpful. Forewarned is forearmed. I don't want her to be afraid to fall in love with someone."

"I'm glad you agree. And thank you for the dinner invitation."

When they walked into the café, Martin requested a table in the back corner. Tonight he wanted to spend the evening just with Laura. When he wasn't concentrating on work, his thoughts often turned to her and lingered there.

In mid-May 1898, Martin arranged a small celebration for Nellie's graduation. "Nellie, tonight Laura and the McGranes will join us for supper at The Breakfast House to celebrate your graduation from secondary school."

"Thanks, Papa. That will be a nice evening."

"Yes, it will. Also, there's something I want to discuss with you. James telephoned this morning and asked if you were still interested in working at McCann's law office. He said his offer of having you live with them still stood. I told him I'd talk to you about it and let him know.

"Assuming you still want to move to Cheyenne, here's what I'm proposing until next spring. How about spending half the day assisting me on basic legal tasks and then reading your law books the rest of the day? If we do that, you should be ready to do some basic work in McCann's office by next summer."

Nellie threw her arms around Martin. "Papa, that would be perfect."

"I'm not trying to push you out the door, but I don't want to hold you back from what you're meant to do. Also, I think it's time for you to get some new clothes. I'll ask Laura to help you. I think you should definitely buy a long buckskin skirt and some new boots. Whatever else you buy is up to you two."

In late June, a young man walked into their office. Before the man said anything, Martin noticed he did a double take when he saw Nellie and she also gave him a quick second look. He'd never seen her look at a man like that.

"Good morning. My name is John Groen."

Martin stood up. "Good morning. I'm Martin Handshoe. How can I help you?"

"I'm actually on my way to Cheyenne, but I stopped here at the request of Willem Van Dyke, a close friend in Iowa. He has been trying to locate his older brother Martin for quite a while and thinks he might live in this part of South Dakota.

"The family last saw Martin in 1868 when he took their cattle to the Chicago stockyards. He never returned home but, after several years, they started receiving wire transfers from Wyoming and then from this area. When I told Willem I was leaving for Cheyenne, he asked me to stop in the Black Hills and see if I could find his brother. This was the last location from which a wire transfer was sent. If you don't have any suggestions, I'll check around Cheyenne once I get there."

After watching Martin, Hakáta took a protective stance beside him. Nellie was also trying to decipher the expression on his face.

"I seem to have upset all of you. I apologize. I was just trying to help my friend." John nodded and turned to leave.

"Please don't leave," Martin said. "I am Willem's brother. I just wasn't expecting this. Nellie, would you please make some tea while I rearrange the chairs? This conversation might take a while." He pulled three chairs around the small table near the back of the office.

"I think it's better if you listen to my story first. Then I'll answer any questions you might have. When I was in seventh grade, I had to drop off some documents at a small law firm in Pella. That was the day I decided to become a lawyer. After I graduated from secondary school, I worked part-time at the law firm and part-time on our farm. My father promised me I could work at the law office full-time after our farm was paid off.

"In the summer of 1868, he assigned me to take our cattle to the Chicago stockyards. With the money from that sale, our family would finally own our land outright. A direct rail line to the Chicago stockyards passed through town, so everything should have been straightforward.

"Before I boarded the train, my mother pulled me aside, placed a small silk sack in my hand, and said, 'Take this for your protection. I pray Oma Magdalena's pendant will keep you safe. I wish you were not traveling alone. I will not be at peace until you return home.' I put it in my shirt pocket and buttoned the flap. Nellie, this is the amber pendant you wear every day."

Nellie clasped the gemstone and blinked back tears.

"The cattle sale went according to plan. By midafternoon I was walking back to the train station when I was attacked and robbed by two men. One slammed brass knuckles across my face while the other ripped open the inner pocket of my jacket and grabbed the sale documents. If not for an old man in a horse-drawn wagon, I'm sure they would have killed me. After he fired several shots at them, they ran off.

"The old gentleman took me to the train depot and advised me to climb into an empty boxcar so I could save some money. Most of the boxcars were empty, heading back west for more cattle, so I climbed into what I thought was an empty car and leaned back into one of the corners.

"After the train left the stockyards, I noticed a young man sitting in the opposite corner from me. I nodded to him, and he did the same. I detected nothing threatening about him. My mother had stuffed some biscuits and sausage into my satchel, and I offered to share them with the stranger. Nellie, the man turned out to be James. When we started talking, he explained that he'd fought for the North in the Civil War. After the war, when he returned to the family farm in Missouri, his brother, who'd fought for the South, threw him off the farm."

Nellie turned to John Groen. "James is my father's best friend who lives in Cheyenne."

"In June 1876, I accepted an offer to go on a cattle drive to the Black Hills," Martin continued. "Andrew Sanborn, the man who hired me, wanted to establish a cattle ranch in the Spearfish area. I worked for him until I was hired by the lawyer who started this law firm. Sanborn is one of my closest friends here."

"This is all very intriguing. Your oldest brother and my father are good friends."

Martin smiled. "Life weaves quite an interesting pattern, doesn't it? How is my brother Jan?"

"He's a very successful farmer, as is your youngest brother Willem. Your brother Dirk, the difficult one, died in a hunting accident about five years after you left."

Martin nodded. He didn't want to know the details. That evening, the three of them had supper at The Breakfast House.

It was a pleasant evening, with Nellie and John Groen carrying most of the conversation. There were several businesses for sale in Cheyenne, and he was looking to buy one of them. Early the next morning, he took the first train to Cheyenne.

13

IN EARLY SEPTEMBER, MARTIN AND NELLIE WERE going over some legal documents when a stranger entered the office. Something about him looked familiar to Martin, but he couldn't lock in on it. Hakáta came to Martin's side, her ears erect and her eyes trained on the man.

Martin stood up. "Good afternoon. Could I help you with something?"

"I am Willem Van Dyke, your youngest brother. When John Groen sent me a letter about his visit with a Martin Handshoe, I knew it had to be you."

"I didn't think I would ever see you again." Martin swallowed hard, then clasped Willem's shoulders. "This is your niece, Nellie. The three of us can sit around that table near the window. Would you like something to drink? Tea? Coffee?"

"Thank you. Some tea would be nice."

When Martin returned with the tea, Hakáta was sitting in front of Willem with a paw on one of his knees. "Willem, I've never seen her do that with a stranger."

"She's a good judge of character, Papa," Nellie said.

Martin smiled. "Yes, she is." When he looked again at Willem, Hakáta was letting him pet her.

"I wanted to find you for several reasons. The first one is to tell you that Mother passed away in July. She never stopped believing in her Martyn."

Martin blinked and looked away for a few moments. "Did

198

she pass on July twentieth?"

"Yes. How did you know that?"

"I woke up early that morning. Many times over the years I've sensed her presence, but that morning it felt different. It felt like a farewell."

Willem nodded. "I never questioned her love for me, but her love for you ran deeper than it did for the rest of us."

"I'm not so sure about that."

"Well, we can agree to disagree on that subject. When your wire transfers started arriving, it comforted Mother to know you were somewhere safe. The restitution you made to our family over the years must have surpassed the amount that was stolen from you. On her deathbed, Mother asked me to find you and let you know we received your payments. She also said to tell you she never stopped loving you."

Martin blinked away tears.

"So this June, after John Groen arrived in Cheyenne, he sent me a long letter about his visit here. He explained about the robbery near the Chicago stockyards and how you ended up in Cheyenne. When he said you were now practicing law in Spearfish, I decided to find you. How did you meet Nellie's mother?"

"In 1878, an older lawyer took me under his wing and accepted me into his practice in Spearfish. Three years later I was in Deadwood on business when I saw the most beautiful woman I'd ever laid eyes on. As soon as she stepped off the stagecoach, the owner of one of the saloons approached her. She looked so frightened. I took her aside and explained what kind of man he was. She said the train ticket had taken almost all of her money.

"I asked her what she'd spent on the ticket and gave that amount to her. Then I offered to bring her to Spearfish and have her stay with close friends—the Episcopal minister and his wife—until she decided what she wanted to do. I knew they wouldn't refuse to take her in. I also made it clear she was under no obligation to me.

"When we rode through the Spearfish River Canyon, she started to calm down and told me why she'd fled from Missouri to Deadwood. Her older sister had taken her in after both their parents passed in a flu epidemic. Several months later, her brother-in-law started getting a bit aggressive with her. Adrianna was terrified of him. Late one afternoon, her sister shoved some money into Adrianna's pocket along with advertisements for women to work in Deadwood's saloons. She said she feared for Adrianna's safety.

"That evening, she went to bed early and escaped as soon as it was dark. She walked to town and hid in a corner of the train station. As soon as the station opened the next morning, she bought a ticket and was on her way to the Black Hills.

"She lived with Reverend David and Rebekah McGrane until we were married the following spring. Nellie was born a year later. We were so wonderfully happy. When Nellie turned four years old, we were expecting our second child. Adrianna's pregnancy was normal until she went into labor. As soon as her labor started, something seemed different. When I brought the midwife to our home, she took one look at Adrianna and said I should get her doctor. I took Nellie with me, left her with the McGranes, and had the doctor follow me home.

"Within an hour he took me aside and told me to get our minister. Nellie and I lost Adrianna and the baby that night."

"I'm so sorry, Martin."

"Papa, I'd like to tell the story about how we found Hakáta," Nellie said.

Martin nodded.

"Several months after Mama and my baby sister passed away, Papa and I were walking in the woods behind our house. It was a cold fall day. I heard a little crying sound and stopped to see where it was coming from. First I saw a dead wolf, then I noticed a cub beside her.

"Papa was ahead of me so I called to him to come back.

He wasn't happy about it but he let me bring the cub home. Tuŋkášila, my Lakota grandfather, said I should name her Hakáta. It means 'little sister' in Lakota. She is my protector, but she's getting a bit old now."

"You're very fortunate to have her," Willem noted, to which Nellie nodded.

"Nellie inherited her beautiful hair from Adrianna," Martin said.

"But I believe she has Mother's eyes."

Martin smiled. "Willem, I think you're right." He looked at Nellie. She was too choked up to say anything.

"Is that Oma Magdalena's brooch Nellie is wearing?"

Martin nodded. "When I fled west on that train from Chicago, I opened the sack of food Mother had packed for me and found an envelope beneath the food. The brooch was inside it and also a note saying she hoped the brooch would protect me until I returned home."

Martin noticed Nellie looking down, gently touching the brooch.

After decades of protecting his identity, Martin's defenses crumbled. Looking at Willem, he searched for the face of his ten-year-old brother and found a handsome man, a shock of auburn hair still falling across his forehead. Throughout his childhood, Willem had always been without guile. His clear blue eyes still reflected the truth he carried within him.

"Before Adrianna came into my life, I developed a deep friendship with a Lakota. His name was White Wolf, and I owe my life to him. When I first came to the Black Hills, I worked on a cattle ranch while I continued to read the law. Out on the range, I often had the sensation that someone or something was watching me. One day I was searching for a stray and sat down on a boulder to eat some hard tack. Before I could comprehend what was happening, a bullet flew past my ear and hit the rock. The bullet killed a rattle snake that was about to strike me.

"I flew to my feet and saw a Lakota standing about thirty feet from me. I asked him if he spoke some English, and he nodded. We became good friends and often hunted and fished together.

"After Adrianna and I were married, there were times I had to stay overnight in Deadwood. I don't know how White Wolf knew I was gone, but he'd arrive late in the day, eat supper with Adrianna and sleep on our front porch. He always left before daybreak. Adrianna trusted and admired White Wolf. After Nellie was born, he became like a grandfather to her."

"Martin, do you remember our family dog, the one that loved you above everyone else?"

"Yes, of course."

"Every day, starting with the day you took the train to Chicago, he walked to the end of our lane and stopped when he reached the road. Until the day he passed, he spent every afternoon there waiting for you to come home."

"That makes me sad. He was such a gentle dog. How long will you be able to stay with us?"

"Four or five nights if that would be all right."

"That would be wonderful. You're welcome to stay longer. We'll explore the Black Hills with you and show you Devil's Tower in Wyoming."

One week later, when Martin was going through the mail, he noticed a letter addressed to Nellie from John Groen. She was out meeting someone for coffee, so he set it on her desk, smiling to himself.

When Nellie returned to the office, she immediately opened the letter. "Papa, John Groen purchased an outfitting shop for western gear and clothing. He said he'd be pleased to see me if I ever come to Cheyenne. Do you think we could go there before the weather turns cold? I would also like to stop by McCann's law office."

"Yes, we could do that. It would be good for you to meet with McCann and let him know how your studies are going. You should also explain the legal assistance you've been providing me. I'll arrange a hotel room for us. Oh, and you should also probably stop by John Groen's shop."

Nellie rolled her eyes. "Since you insist, I'll be sure to do that."

"I'll send Doc Matheson a telegram and see if we can spend an afternoon on his ranch."

"That would be wonderful."

In late September, Martin and Nellie took a train to Cheyenne. After getting settled in their hotel room, they walked to John Groen's shop. Martin stayed for a short time, then left to spend the rest of the afternoon with James.

The next morning, he and Nellie went to McCann's office for a couple of hours. Before they left, McCann pulled Martin aside. "Our staff is backlogged. Could you please spend two days here after you go to Doc's ranch? Also, I'm impressed with Nellie's diligence in handling the tasks I assigned her today. She learns quickly."

"She loves reading the law, perhaps even more than I did. She's chomping at the bit to work for your firm."

"What kind of time frame are you thinking about?"

"I was thinking early next year."

"Actually, we could use her right now to help with basic research and documents. Don't answer me this moment. Just think about it. Also, would you ever consider moving back here and working for the firm again? We could definitely use your expertise."

"Thank you. You've caught me a bit off guard. I'm not ready to do that right now, but I'd appreciate being able to revisit it at a later date. Nellie and I are going to spend a night at Doc's ranch. I'll see you again before we leave."

After they returned from Doc's ranch, the situation shifted

rapidly. Martin and Nellie met with McCann and arranged for Nellie to start working for his firm by mid-October. McCann didn't press hard, but he again asked Martin to consider moving to Cheyenne if someone ever bought out his practice.

Once they were back in Spearfish, Nellie had two weeks to prepare for her move to Cheyenne. She sorted through her belongings, setting aside only what she absolutely needed to take with her. The day before she left, Martin drove their wagon to the massacre site where they honored White Wolf each year. Hakáta sat between Nellie and Martin, no longer able to run any great distance. They tied prayer strips on the pine branches, shared their memories of him, and then sat quietly for quite some time. Laura had supper with them that evening.

Nellie's move to Cheyenne forced Martin to accept that he was no longer responsible for her. Another consequence was that it allowed his and Laura's relationship to deepen into an adult relationship. They usually had supper at one of the cafés and then returned to Laura's house. Oftentimes he didn't head home until just before daybreak. Martin felt a sense of peace growing inside him. Each of them, for their own reasons, was in no rush to commit to anything legal.

In January 1899, a powerful winter storm blew out of the Rockies, sinking temperatures to record lows and leaving two-to three-foot drifts of snow in its wake. When Martin finally managed to clear his way to the barn the next morning, he found Blaze and Hakáta frozen to death. He felt relieved that Nellie wasn't there to witness it. Rationally he knew they'd both outlived their projected lifetimes, but that didn't prevent a deep sense of loss from enveloping him.

Martin bundled up with extra layers and trudged into town. First, he checked in with Laura to make sure she was safe. Then he arranged for Blaze and Hakáta's remains to be moved to the woods. He felt exhausted and sad. With the dislocation caused by the blizzard, it would take at least a day for him to find a new horse. Late that afternoon, he went to see Laura after she'd closed her office and didn't leave until early morning. There was no longer a need for him to rush back home.

One year later, in February 1900, Martin received a letter from John Groen. He opened it, read it slowly, then read it again. Groen was asking for Martin's blessing to marry Nellie. The letter was written respectfully and left no doubt about his devotion to her. Martin responded immediately, giving Groen his blessing and sending his best wishes. He also wrote Nellie to tell her how happy he was for the two of them.

Two weeks later, Martin received a letter from Nellie requesting Martin and Laura's presence at their wedding in mid-May. That evening, he showed Laura the letter. "Do you think you could take some time off to come to Cheyenne with me? It would mean so much to Nellie and me if you could attend the wedding. Also, I'd like to show you around the town."

"I would love to do that. I'll arrange for someone to be on call."

After the wedding, they stayed an extra day in Cheyenne so they could visit Doc Matheson and Etta. On the return train ride to Spearfish, Martin placed his hand over Laura's. "What did you think of Cheyenne?"

"I found it very interesting. It's much bigger than I'd expected. What I enjoyed the most, aside from the wedding, was meeting James and Anna and also Doc and Etta."

"Do you think you could ever consider living in Cheyenne? I'm in no rush, but I'm thinking of selling my practice in a year or two. McCann continues to stress that he'd like me to join his firm."

"Let's discuss that at a later date. I have a well-established practice. I'm not quite sure how I would fit into that picture."

Martin could have kicked himself. What was he thinking? Laura had worked long and hard to establish her medical practice. He couldn't expect her to walk away from it. She was a very independent woman. After her disastrous first marriage, he wasn't sure how she felt about marrying again. One of Martin's friends advised him, "If it ain't broke, don't fix it."

In 1903, Martin received an offer to buy out his practice, too sweet an offer to refuse. Certain that he'd never receive that kind of offer again, he agreed to continue working at his firm for one more year to ensure an orderly transition. That evening, after they returned from eating supper, Laura made tea for them.

"Martin, you seem a bit distracted."

"You know me so well. This morning Will Jones made an offer to buy out my practice. It's a generous amount, more than I ever dreamed of being offered."

"And you accepted his offer."

"Yes, I did."

"Well, I knew it was only a matter of time before this would happen. I understand why you're doing this. You need to be near Nellie. It would be foolish to turn down a generous offer for your practice. You've worked hard and shouldered a lot of responsibility to make this happen."

"I agreed to stay on for a year to finish any cases I'm working on and to assist Will. About twelve to eighteen months from now, I'll start working for McCann's practice."

That pretty much ended the conversation. Martin sensed the tension between them and decided it was better to stop before he dug a deeper hole. After that evening, things were never quite the same between him and Laura. They still continued to spend time together, and he usually spent the night at her place, but there was a strain in their relationship that hadn't been there before.

Martin moved to Cheyenne in May 1905 and started working for McCann immediately. He and Nellie usually spent time together over the noon hour, confirming his decision that leaving Spearfish was the right thing to do. About two months after his arrival, Nellie told him she and John were expecting their first child in February.

Martin was thrilled with her news. He wanted to share it with Laura but, because of the tension between them, decided a letter would be the best way to inform her. He missed her presence in his life. She was on his mind the first thing when he awakened and the last thing before he fell asleep. He felt miserable about the way they had parted.

In February, Nellie gave birth to a healthy baby boy. They named him Robert after John's favorite uncle. When Nellie placed the baby in Martin's hands, he was overwhelmed with emotion and filled with thanksgiving that little Robert was a healthy baby. He still hoped that one day Laura would move to Cheyenne. He and Nellie often discussed how to make that happen but hadn't found a solution.

Martin didn't know what he would do without James and Anna's presence in his life. His social life revolved around them and Nellie's family. James and Anna frequently invited him over for supper, and Martin reciprocated by treating them to the local restaurants. He just wished Laura could be part of his life too.

Almost a year later, Martin took a train to Spearfish. He had a week's worth of legal work he needed to tackle and hoped there wouldn't be a winter storm. Equally important, he wanted to have a long-overdue conversation with Laura. He thought about calling her office phone but then decided it would be better to just show up on her doorstep. If he caught her off guard, maybe she wouldn't refuse to invite him inside.

The train got a late start and arrived just after sunset. When Martin knocked on her office door, Laura opened the door partway, clearly startled to see him.

"Hello, Laura."

"Well, this is quite unexpected."

"I thought it might be better to surprise you, in case you'd want to avoid seeing me. I have a few things I'd like to discuss with you."

She opened the door wider and he stepped inside. She wasn't smiling.

"I have missed you so very much."

"Sit down. I'll make some tea."

Something about her manner kept Martin from saying anything else. He sat at her kitchen table and watched her heat water for the tea. She focused on the task with her usual concentration. It was the way she approached everything, nothing done halfway. The tenderness of the moment made him catch his breath. He wanted to live out his life with her at his side.

She brought the teapot to the table and poured tea for them. "Martin, this has been a difficult day for me. It began at five o'clock this morning with Peter Hanson pounding on my front door. He said their fourteen-year-old son Jonah was very sick.

"I rushed to get my medical bag. A serious influenza has been working its way through the community. When Peter took me to their home, Jonah was having difficulty breathing. I remained there until midafternoon when he passed. There was nothing I could do. I've known him since he was very young. He was an exceptional child—generous, intelligent, kind. He seemed interested in becoming a doctor. I had dreamed that maybe someday he would take over my practice. Why are those who have so much to give—to their families, to the world—often taken so early? It's the same thing that happened with your Adrianna. I'm exhausted. Too exhausted to talk tonight."

"How about the two of us just stretching out on that big sofa of yours so I can hold you beside me the rest of the night?" He was sure she slept on this sofa many an evening.

Martin stretched out along the back of the sofa, pulled her next to him, and draped a heavy woolen blanket over them. What a selfish fool he'd been to not recognize how exhausted she was. How could he not have noticed the sadness that filled her eyes?

"I love you, Laura."

But she didn't hear him. She was already asleep.

The next morning, Martin extricated himself from the sofa, stuffed the blanket around Laura, and made coffee. When he brought a cup to her, Laura sat up and stayed wrapped in the blanket.

"I woke up several times last night. It gave me great comfort to feel your arm across me. I felt safe. The loss of Jonah weighs heavily on me."

"After Adrianna passed, I was deeply wounded. Have you ever loved someone so much that you couldn't imagine being with anyone else?"

"No, I have not." Laura looked directly into his eyes. "I thought my former husband loved me but there was no great love between us. He liked the money my practice brought in."

"After Adrianna passed, I felt numb. I couldn't imagine ever loving someone again. But that has changed. These past eighteen months, I've missed you so very much. I begin and end each day thinking about you, wishing we were together.

To be honest, whenever I'm not busy, you're in my thoughts.

"I can't compare the love I felt for Adrianna with what I feel for you. I'm older. The love I feel for you runs like a deep river. If you will have me, I would like to spend the rest of my life with you. I promise to protect you and cherish you."

Laura stared at him.

"I apologize. I've caught you off guard. I should have planned this better or at least given you time to wake up."

"Martin, I have been captivated with you for a very long time. When we met, I could tell you had no room in your heart for another woman. I decided that, if the most that could ever develop between us was a deep adult relationship, I would be thankful for that. When you left for Wyoming, I gave up hope of ever having a lasting relationship with you. So you see, this sleepyhead is a bit surprised with your proposal. As for my answer, I would love to spend the rest of my life with you. The only complication is my practice."

She nestled against his shoulder and wrapped an arm across his chest. After a bit, they moved to the kitchen table and had another cup of coffee.

"I have a lawsuit I need to work on in Deadwood and will be here for five days. Then I'll have to return to Cheyenne. I'll come here each afternoon as soon as I can." He pulled what looked like a legal document out of his briefcase. "I made a list of all the reasons I love you and want to be with you. Please read it sometime today so we can discuss it tonight. Also, Nellie asked me to deliver this letter to you. I have no idea what she has written, but I expect it's an appeal for you to move to Cheyenne."

When Martin returned late that afternoon, Laura hung the "Closed" sign on her shop door. "In your list of reasons why you love me, I also found a list of doctors who would like to expand their practices in Cheyenne, especially if the candidate is a woman.

"And that isn't all. Nellie and John are expecting a baby

in the fall. I'm sure they would welcome having grandparents around to give them a bit of relief from time to time."

"I'm not sure how soon I could sell my practice," Laura said. "Last week I received an inquiry from a recent medical school graduate who is thinking about moving here. I had delayed responding to him. I'll write him today. If he were to decide to buy out my practice, and that's not a given, I'd want to stay here until he felt comfortable with assuming full responsibility for it."

"That sounds good. We don't have to wait to marry until you move to Cheyenne. Let's go over to the McGranes' this afternoon and talk to Reverend David about setting a date for our wedding. I think we should have a celebration in the church hall afterward with all our friends. I'll come back here two or three weekends each month until you move to Cheyenne."

"Hmmm. Is there anything else you've decided?"

"No, that's about it. But I'm still waiting for you to say yes."

Laura smiled and placed her hand over his. "Yes, Martin."

Afterword

THE SIOUX NATION NEVER ACCEPTED THE FORCED DIS-
possession of their Black Hills reservation in 1877. A century
later in 1978, after repeated attempts to address this issue,
Sioux lobbyists convinced the U.S. Congress to pass a law giving authority to the U.S. Claims Court to hear their case without regard to *res judicata*—a case already decided.

On July 3, 1980, in *United States v. Sioux Nation of Indians*, the
U.S. Supreme Court, having reviewed the fifty-seven-year-old
Black Hills claims case of the Great Sioux Reservation, ruled
that Congress had failed to give the Sioux the full value of
their land. The ruling stated that, while Congress has para-
mount authority over Indian property, "Congress acts properly only if it makes a good faith effort to give the Indians
the full value of their land." The Supreme Court determined
this had not been done and ordered that just compensation
be given to the Sioux Nation, including an award of interest.

The Sioux have refused to accept the award because acceptance would legally terminate Sioux demands for the return
of the Black Hills. The sum, uncollected and accruing interest,
now exceeds $1 billion. The Sioux Nation would rather have
the Black Hills than monetary compensation.

About Atmosphere Press

Founded in 2015, Atmosphere Press was built on the principles of Honesty, Transparency, Professionalism, Kindness, and Making Your Book Awesome. As an ethical and author-friendly hybrid press, we stay true to that founding mission today.

If you're a reader, enter our giveaway for a free book here:

SCAN TO ENTER
BOOK GIVEAWAY

If you're a writer, submit your manuscript for consideration here:

SCAN TO SUBMIT
MANUSCRIPT

And always feel free to visit Atmosphere Press and our authors online at atmospherepress.com. See you there soon!

About the Author

After the Civil War, a distant relative of Jane Iwan's was designated to sell his family's cattle at the Chicago Stockyards. The proceeds from that sale were intended be pay off the homestead loan, giving the family outright ownership of prime farmland. There was only one problem: the son who was responsible for selling the cattle never returned home, resulting in the loss of the family farm.

Since she was a child, Jane Iwan has always wondered what really happened. Perhaps the cousin actually sold the cattle and then absconded with the money. She researched various websites and records, all to no avail. Long fascinated with the American West, Iwan decided to create her own account of what might have occurred.

www.ingramcontent.com/pod-product-compliance
Lightning Source LLC
Chambersburg PA
CBHW021524150726
47990CB00006B/2080